Rusty Wilson's

....

More
Bigfoot
Campfire
Stories

It always amazes me how the quietest person can often have the scariest tale. I think Bigfoot is attracted to thinkers. —*Rusty Wilson*

Contents

i   Foreword, *by Rusty Wilson*

1   The Bigfoot Ghost Town

15   Sleeping with the Enemy

26   The Intruder

39   Bigfoot Potluck

52   Pumped Up at the Pump Jack

62   The Windigo of Grand Mesa

76   Just One Little Drink

93   Sarah's Bigfoot Boat Float

105   The Night Hikers

110   The Hounds of Mist

126   At the Office

139   Mexican Mountain Madness

159   The Bigfoot Drive-Through

170   The Revelation

178   Bigfoot Cassidy and the Great Train Crash

188   Runaway Bigfoot Ramp

196   The Back Forty

208   About the Author

Foreword

. . . .

by Rusty Wilson

Greetings, fellow adventurers, to this new volume of Bigfoot campfire stories. If you've read the first book of this collection, you'll know that you're in for a treat if you enjoy Bigfoot and adventure, and most people who love one also love the other.

These stories were collected around many campfires, where my flyfishing clients regaled and scared me to death with their Bigfoot encounters. It always amazes me how the quietest person can often have the scariest tale—I think Bigfoot is attracted to thinkers, or maybe the meek shall inherit Bigfoot.

So, pull up a chair or log, kick back with some hot chocolate, and be prepared to read some tales that will make your hair stand on end—or maybe make you wonder if you might like to meet the Big Guy himself.

[1] The Bigfoot Ghost Town

· ·

The first story in this collection was told by a retired fellow named Wally. He was a real storyteller who had us all on the edge of our seats—or I should say logs. We were sitting around a campfire not too far from where the story took place, in my home state of Colorado, not far from Steamboat Springs and where the little town of Mt. Harris once stood.

Wally had been on several of my guide trips and always just sat there real quiet and listened when the campfire tales got going. I had no idea he had such a good story of his own, but he's kind of a thinker type, and I guess it took him awhile to work up to telling it. I'm glad he did.

When I was a kid, my friend and I discovered a Bigfoot ghost town. Before you laugh, let me tell the story, and maybe you'll agree it could be true.

I'm Wally, and my best friend growing up was Ralphie. We grew up in the small town of Steamboat Springs, Colorado. Maybe you've heard of it, as it's a famous ski town in the northwest part of the state. It was the birthplace of ski jumping in the United States, but that was before my time.

I was a kid there before the ski industry really took off, so we learned to ski by hiking up the hills or having horses pull us around. It was a lot of fun, but way different than what's there today, a lot smaller, too. When I was young, it had only about 2,000 people.

Steamboat was named for the hot springs that would blow off and sound like a steamboat whistle. That was also before my time. When they brought the railroad through, they blasted out the rocks that created the whistle in order to put the tracks through there.

The area still has lots of hot springs, and I grew up swimming in the hot springs pool there. It was fun to go there on a cold winter day and sit in the warm water while it snowed. We felt like royalty, sitting there in the steam and strong smell of sulfur.

My parents both worked, my mom at the grocery store and my dad at the local auto shop, so I had lots of time to get into mischief. I had lots of great adventures, but the ghost town was the most unique, without a doubt.

Ralphie and I spent every waking moment together during the summer. We were best pals. We liked to bicycle around everywhere and explore.

We ended up in some pretty crazy places, like the time we rode to the top of Rabbit Ears Pass and Ralphie's brakes went out, or the time we rode all the way to Hayden and had to call my uncle to come get us—that was a good 30 mile ride, and we're talking old clunker bicycles. Of course, he was sworn to secrecy and never told my parents.

So, for us to ride down to Mt. Harris, a good 15 miles one way, was a good day's ride, but not unusual. We would pack a lunch and just take off all day. It was a great way to grow up.

Mt. Harris was an old abandoned coal mining town just across the Yampa River from the highway. There was an old bridge crossing that was kind of scary, as you could see the river through the planks, then you crossed a small area full of cattails and willows, so you had to stay on the road.

Then you were in the old town, which was kind of along the hillside, climbing right up by the cliffs where the old coal mine had been. I don't know when it was operational, but way before our time.

At the time we were there, it was already pretty much a ghost town, and a lot of the buildings were in serious disrepair, with roofs caving in and windows broken out.

A number of the better constructed houses had been moved by locals to the neighboring towns. Hayden, Craig, Milner, even Steamboat all had old Mt. Harris houses that had been moved years before and refurbished for people to live in.

You could tell a Mt. Harris house because they were all the same—square with a peaked roof and wide wood plank siding. The town's little school had been moved up by Craig, some 35 miles away, where it was used as a rural school. They even moved the old desks.

So, me and Ralphie would go to Mt. Harris when we felt ambitious enough for the bike ride and explore around. Sometimes we would sit up there on the hill and watch the occasional train go by, which wasn't very occasional, as the tracks ended in Craig.

We would go up there on an average of once or twice a month in the summer. It was our own secret town, even though it was falling down. We liked to pretend we ran it, and we'd run off outlaws and bankers alike in our imaginary escapades there.

Then one day in late July, everything changed. We had packed our lunches and headed for our town, eager to run off some imaginary squatters we'd heard had come in. Rumor was they were looking for gold and planned on taking over the town.

Of course, this was all part of a story we'd made up on the way out there to give the day some excitement.

We crossed the old bridge, and I immediately stopped, yelling at Ralphie, who had gone on up the road towards the old town. He turned around and came back.

"Ralphie, stop and be quiet here for a minute. Something's different, but I don't know what."

Ralphie stopped and grinned, thinking I was coming up with some plot or whatever to liven up the day. We stood there, but all we could hear was the rustling of the river as it went on down towards Hayden and Craig.

Ralphie soon lost his grin, though, and he eyed me suspiciously. "Wally, you're just tryin' to get me worked up, I know it," he said. "But something does feel different. What is it?"

"I dunno, but things just don't feel right. I'm not makin' anything up, it just feels different."

We stood there for a bit and even discussed turning around and going on home. We both had a sensation that things were different, not necessarily bad, but different, and we couldn't put our finger on what it could be or why.

But we both felt it. And the longer we stood there, the more defined it became, until we both felt like we were being watched.

"This is creepy," Ralphie said. "It feels like there's someone or something watchin' us. It's makin' the hairs on my arms stand up."

"Yeah, mine too," I agreed. "Maybe we should just go home. Maybe there's a mountain lion up there or a bear or something."

Ralphie looked pained. He didn't want to go home, the day was young, yet he was a bit scared, as was I. Maybe our imaginary squatters weren't so imaginary. He figured out a solution.

"I know, Wally, let's act like we're leaving. That will throw whatever it is off, then let's come back down the river in the willows and hideout and spy. We'll be on the other side of the river so nothin' can get to us, but we can get pretty close."

This sounded like a good plan, though I was feeling a bit like we should just leave. So, we turned around and crossed back over the bridge and rode on back up the highway for a good half-mile, then hid our bikes in the bushes and snuck back along the river in the willows.

Our escapade was getting to be more serious than we'd planned, as we both had the feeling we could be in actual danger, especially if a wild animal were on to us.

Of course, I later found out that cougars and bears usually go the opposite way of humans, but at the time, we thought we could even be stalked or something.

We snuck back up almost to the bridge, where we could see up to the old town. We hid in some sumac, all scratched to heck from all the wild rose bushes along the river.

We were persistent, determined to figure out who had taken over "our" town. We even mentioned that since it was a ghost town, maybe some real ghosts had discovered it and moved in. You know how kids are, we managed to scare ourselves with every suggestion we could think of.

So there we were, hiding in the bushes, spying on the town of which not so long ago we'd been mayor and sheriff and ruled with an iron hand.

We sat for awhile, and the creepy feeling of being watched was gone, everything seemed normal again. We whispered some, deciding we must have imagined the whole thing. We grinned at each other at the power of our imaginations in kind of a proud way.

"Maybe we should go get our bikes and go on up there," Ralphie suggested.

Just then, a rancid smell drifted down from the old town, almost making us gag. It was like a mix between garbage and a skunk. At the same time, I saw something move behind one of the old houses. I grabbed Ralphie's arm and pointed. His eyes got big when he saw it, too.

"A bear!" he whispered excitedly. "A big big black bear, and it's big."

Now we saw another, and it appeared the two were talking or something, as they were facing each other, gesticulating as if having a conversation. We were too far away to hear anything. They were huge, standing on their rear legs, maybe nine feet tall and 600 or 700 pounds. They were thick through the torso and their hair was rusty-reddish brown, sort of like an Irish Setter's.

A feeling of dread overcame me.

"I'm getting out of here. Let's go."

We both ran like the wind through the bushes, never looking back, got to our bikes and made record time back to town, which was uphill part way.

We stopped at my house, since it was closest, puffing and my heart beating like I'd never felt before. I thought maybe I was going to have a heart attack at the ripe old age of 13.

We lay on the garage floor, trying to regain our senses, still scared.

"Do you think they might have followed us?" Ralphie asked.

"No way," I answered authoritatively, though I wondered myself. I was afraid to sleep alone in my room for a few days after that, instead sleeping on the couch in the living room.

We had many discussions in the following days about what we'd seen, but it always came back to having been bears. Keep in mind that at this time Bigfoot was not a common topic and existed only in Canada or the Pacific Northwest.

We rolled it around and around, trying to figure out what these really big bears would be doing in Mt. Harris, and did bears really talk to each other and use their hands—uh oh, wait, these things had hands! Our discussions were getting more and more afield from bears, and we still couldn't explain it.

We needed to go back and do more spying so we could rest easy. One more look, and we could establish once and for all that they were just bears hanging out, maybe using the old buildings for shelter, checking them out for hibernation places, you know how bears are.

Maybe some Alaskan Kodiak bears had come into the area, migrated, cause these weren't like any black bears we'd seen, and there were no grizzlies around, plus these guys didn't have humps like grizzlies, and only Kodiak bears were that big.

We had stumbled onto a full-blown mystery, and were we men enough to solve it, or were we just going to keep playing cowboy and outlaw games like kids? We asked ourselves these questions until we finally worked up enough courage to go back, even though it took several days of false starts.

We would pack lunches and get ready to go, then something more pressing would come up, like needing to return books to the library or go check out the new bikes at the hardware store, that kind of thing.

Finally, the day came when we could procrastinate no longer, because school would start tomorrow. We had to go now, or the mystery would haunt us forever. We would no longer be able to claim our place in history as brave explorers, but would go down as cowards.

We took off, riding slow. I think we set a record for slowest ride that day, except we made up for it on the way back, which probably beat even our last return as fastest ride ever. But we solved the mystery, and we paid a price for that.

At least we no longer felt like cowards, but by then, being a coward was no honor lost. We wished we had been bigger cowards.

We got to the place where we'd left our bikes in the bushes before. This time we hid them so well we almost couldn't find them in our panic on the way back.

We snuck down the same route along the river, but this time even more quietly, as we knew we were dealing with something potentially life-threatening, whereas before, we weren't sure.

But now we had secret weapons—binoculars. We were scared stiff, but determined to know who had invaded our town, assuming they were still there.

Almost to the spy spot, Ralphie stopped, whispering to me that he'd found something really strange. I nearly stepped on it and ruined it, but he pushed me aside at the last minute.

A track. A really really big track, right there in the sand along the river, well-defined and maybe even fresh. Our tracking skills were a bit sketchy. I put my foot next to it and my foot was dwarfed, and I was a growing boy and wore a size 10.

We just stood there for a bit until I stated the obvious, "That ain't no bear track, Ralphie."

He answered in a barely audible whisper, "I know."

After a few moments, I said, "I think we should go home now. We're dealing with something we can't deal with, Ralphie."

Ralphie answered glumly, "I know."

But instead of turning around, something drove us forward. We were almost to the spy spot, so we went on, settling in and nervously pulling our binoculars out of our packs.

Things were different. Someone had destroyed the bridge. It looked like a bomb had hit it. There wasn't much there to start with, but now the planks dangled into space, almost touching the river. They looked like they'd been ripped apart.

"Holy crap," we both said at the same time.

I wanted to run, but didn't. So did Ralphie, he later admitted, but neither of us wanted to appear to be cowards, even though we definitely were.

We sat there, watching the old townsite, scanning with our binoculars like a couple of war generals checking out the battlefield.

We both saw movement at the same time—something big was squatting by one of the houses and stood up. It was one of the Kodiak bears, and it seemed even bigger than before, now that we could see it better.

With the binoculars, I could see that this one was a burnished brown color, with long hair that seemed to hang off its arms. After it stood up, I could see that its arms hung clear down to its knees, and it was as muscular as any wrestler, even more so. It looked like it worked out about 20 hours a day.

Now it walked around behind the building, and it had a long gait, covering a lot of ground in a few steps, swinging its arms. I could see another coming out, leading a small one by the hand. Then another, like maybe a teenager in size.

They stood there and appeared to be arguing, and when the wind was just right we could barely hear them. It sounded like a combination of a chattering noise and Japanese, if you can picture that, but was neither, a sound of its own.

Now, all of a sudden, the hairs on my neck were standing up, and I had that same strange feeling I was being watched. I looked at Ralphie, and I could tell he felt it too.

We were being watched by something that didn't want us there and maybe had some intent of harming us. But the things up the hill weren't even looking our way.

"Something's spotted us," Ralphie whispered, looking like he was ready to cry. "We need to get out of here now."

I decided it was my chance to prove I was braver than him, so I replied, "Let's stay just a few minutes longer and see what they do. We're far enough away we can outrun them."

I couldn't believe what was coming out of my mouth, as all I really wanted to do was run like hell.

We sat there a few more minutes, watching, totally ignoring our instincts. We would pay, I knew it deep inside, but something kept me there, something more than curiosity and bravado.

I figured one was the mom, because she was leading the young one. She now turned and looked straight in our direction, as if sensing us.

I was the one closest to her, and I suddenly doubled over in pain. It felt like someone had kicked me in the stomach, hard. I couldn't move, and I rolled around on the ground, writhing in pain, trying not to cry out.

Ralphie sat there, dumbfounded, then tried to help me, but he didn't know what to do. I was now moaning in pain, and he kept telling me to be quiet, they'll hear us, be quiet, in a panicky voice.

The pain stopped as suddenly as it started, and I sat up, tears running down my cheeks.

"My god, Ralphie, it felt like she kicked me in the stomach. God, that hurt."

"Wally, I don't know what happened, but those ain't bears, and they made you hurt. Let's get outta here."

I took one last look as I got on my feet, just in time to see two of the big creatures running down the hill towards us. But what was worse was that now I could see one coming down the other side of the river towards us, not all that far away.

They were all moving over rocky terrain at a frightening speed. I immediately thought that nothing that big should be able to move that fast.

"Run! Run!" I screamed, no longer trying to be quiet. Ralphie couldn't help but look, and he started screaming, too.

We both ran like the wind, afraid to look back. We knew they had to swim the river, but it looked like something they could do in just a few strokes, or maybe just jump across it in one jump.

I really don't remember anything except riding our bikes back along the highway as fast as we could. We were in a total panic and knew we would die soon. We even tried to wave down the few cars that we saw, but nobody stopped, and we didn't dare stop, either.

We ended up back on the floor of my garage, but this time I was sure I was dying. My stomach hurt like hell, and I couldn't catch my breath.

After he recuperated a bit, Ralphie offered to call my parents or the ambulance or something. He said he sure hated to see me die, who would he hang out with then? And nobody else would believe his story about seeing what we now had deduced were Bigfoot.

He managed to help me get into bed, and I stayed there for a couple of days, telling my folks I had the flu. My stomach was sore for days.

I felt bad lying to my mom, as she thought it was from being sick and brought me all kinds of soups and stuff.

I had nightmares for years, as did Ralphie. The experience kept us together, as nobody on earth would believe us except each other, and we're still close friends after all these years, even though Ralphie now lives 500 miles away. I still live in Steamboat.

The county went out and demolished the town of Mt. Harris years ago, sealing up the old coal mine after they had to rescue a young guy who got stuck in there.

So Mt. Harris is now just a spot where the timber isn't quite as tall, the trees growing where once Ralphie and I had watched a Bigfoot family.

I don't know what became of the Bigfoot, and I don't really want to know. I still have no idea how close we came to being caught or what they would've done to us. I suspect they could have easily caught us and didn't want to.

From other stories I've since heard and read, I think they were just trying to scare us off. And I'm convinced that I was the recipient of a gift of infrasound, with that punch in the stomach.

Sometimes at night I hike up Howelson Hill, the site of the old ski jumps, and look at the stars there above the town. That's about as far out as I'm going to go, knowing what's out there.

[2] Sleeping with the Enemy

This story was the highlight of a long, hard day fishing. It's a tough job, as they say, but someone has to do it. I was guiding a group of five guys, all buddies from the investment business trying to get away from the stress of high achievement and big money. We were at a camp along the Williams Fork River in northwestern Colorado. It was a beautiful spot.

A fellow named Cash told the story, and after hearing it, I decided I needed to get over into Colorado's San Juan Mountains a bit more—but not alone.

I used to do crazy things when I was younger, at least they seem crazy now, though at the time they seemed normal, just something to do. One of these activities was climbing alone, which of course entailed hiking and camping alone to get to the climb.

I thought nothing of loading up my backpack and heading out into some of the most rugged and wild country in the Lower 48 for a week or two, and I often didn't even bother to tell anyone where I was going.

Maybe I had what they call a death wish, but I think it was more like being in denial. I didn't think anything could or would happen to me. I acted like I was invincible, but I wasn't.

One beautiful summer day, I decided to head out for a few days of climbing around the Ice Lakes Basin area near Silverton, Colorado, high in the San Juan Mountains. I had my eye on several peaks, including Golden Horn and Vermilion, both over 13,000 feet.

I knew I would see few, if any, other climbers, as most people were doing the big wall climbs and the Fourteeners, those peaks over 14,000 feet. That left this wild country all to me, though I've heard it's become more crowded in the years since this happened in the mid 1990s.

Ice Lakes Basin is a stiff climb when wearing a backpack, and mine was loaded to the gills. I left my old beater car at the trailhead and took off in mid-afternoon.

I'd hiked the trail before and knew I had time to get to the basin before dark, even though it was steep and a bit hard on the knees when one's loaded down like a pack burro.

I tend to bring everything I might need—I'd rather be prepared than travel light, I guess. I always regretted bringing so much stuff, as I seldom used it all, but the rare time I needed something, I was sure to have it.

I made it to the basin just as darkness fell, and like I predicted, I hadn't seen another soul. Lower and Upper Ice Lakes are both relatively small but glaciated lakes right at timberline, set in a basin beneath some impressive peaks.

I planned to camp the next night at the upper basin, which has an old mining cabin at its edge that has seen better days, though still standing. It was next to Fuller Lake, with Fuller Peak towering above.

In the summer the area is spectacular with wildflowers, including extensive stands of the Colorado state flower, the beautiful blue and white columbine.

I had my little tent up in no time and my stove out with water boiling for a freeze-dried meal of spaghetti. Even freeze-dried stuff tastes good when you're outdoors.

After dinner, I just sat and looked at the stars in amazement. I've never seen stars like what you see in the San Juans. It's a combination of thin atmosphere from the high altitude and clean air, and the sky unfolds layer after layer of stars so thick you feel totally insignificant. It's stunningly beautiful, though humbling.

It's always cold at night when you get into the higher altitudes like that, and even though it was late August, I had on my sweater and down coat and was still a bit chilly.

I was also tired, so I went to bed soon after sunset, which was in itself worth the hike up there, it was so colorful, lots of mares' tails that picked up a wide range of pinks and purples and even oranges. I should have taken more notice that they were mares' tails, but I was tired.

I was sleeping well, which was good, as I sometimes can't sleep at all at altitudes above 11,000 feet, when suddenly I woke with a start.

Crrrraaaaack! Something had just torn apart a big log not far from my tent. Thump—whatever it was then dropped it, making the ground shake.

I had noticed that log earlier, and it was huge, especially considering it was at timberline, where trees struggle to make a living. That log was about three feet across, though not very long. Whatever had picked it up had to be a big strong animal.

My first thought was a bear, as they'll do that, break logs to get at the grubs inside. But it must be a big bear, and there weren't supposed to be anything in this area but black bears, which don't typically get that big.

Maybe it was a remnant grizzly, I thought, as the last known grizzly in the San Juans was killed in the early 1970s. Maybe this one had survived.

The longer I lay there, the more scared I got. If that were a grizz, I could easily be dinner, and this tent would provide absolutely no defense. All I had was my pocket knife, so I would be history.

I could now hear footsteps, and whatever it was, this thing was very heavy, as the ground kind of shook a bit as it walked.

Was it coming my way? God, I was scared. I had to do something, quick.

I really didn't even think about this, it was more a reflexive action, but I sat up and felt around in my pack until I found my little aluminum cooking pan and pulled it out.

I then found a spoon and my headlamp, crawled out of the little tent and turned on the light and started yelling and dancing around in circles while banging on the pan with the spoon and wailing. I did this until I was tired, I don't know, maybe five minutes.

When I stopped, I was out of breath, but I shined my headlamp all around me and saw nothing. After standing there awhile and listening, I crawled back in and went to sleep. Whatever it was, I had obviously out-weirded it.

I woke the next morning to blue skies and immediately went over to investigate the log. Now I was really creeped out, because all around the log were footprints, but they weren't bear prints, but looked like photos I've seen of Bigfoot prints.

I realized I was hyperventilating. I looked all around me, but saw no sign of anything. I had obviously scared it off.

Thinking about that later makes me laugh at the thought that such actions would scare a Bigfoot away, but my ignorance was bliss. It had probably enjoyed the show, thinking about how crazy humans are.

Actually, I wasn't feeling blissful at all, but scared. I didn't even make coffee or breakfast or anything, I just quickly broke camp and stuffed everything in my pack. Time to get out.

I started back down the trail, then stopped. Getting away from the scene made me feel better, and I decided to stop and make breakfast. It was a beautiful sunny bluebird day, why run away? The creature wouldn't bother me now, it was long gone, and it was daylight.

I relaxed a bit and made some freeze-dried eggs and bacon, then coffee. I felt much better—why was I leaving again? Oh, a Bigfoot? Didn't they not exist?

I turned around and went back up the trail. I'd come to climb, and I was nearly there, the hard part was done, getting up to the lower basin. The upper basin wasn't far.

I'd go on up, climb Golden Horn and then decide whether to leave, the day was young. I could still get out by dark if I hustled.

I left my pack by a landmark rock, made up a day pack, and proceeded to climb the mountain. It was aptly named, the top being a glaciated horn. I was excited to make the summit, and I sat there awhile, looking down on Trout Lake on the other side of the drainage. Massive and impressive peaks surrounded me. So many peaks, so little time...

I noticed a bit of a breeze picking up, then could see a thick band of dark clouds to the west. A storm was coming in.

It was then that the previous day's mares' tails clicked, and I realized something big was coming in, not just a small storm. I needed to get out. My decision had been made for me.

By now it was mid-afternoon. I had dawdled a bit and was running behind schedule. I'd planned to get out by dark. But it was still doable, I just needed to get a move on. But you don't want to hurry down a mountain, when you're tired and likely to slip, so it still took awhile before I got back to my pack.

There was no sign of anyone, and the breeze had died down into a stillness that seemed unnatural. I knew it was only a few hours on down to my car, mostly an easy downhill hike, so I made myself a PBJ sandwich and enjoyed what were to be my last moments in the basin.

It was so beautiful, I hated to leave. I pulled out my camera and took some photos, trying to make a panorama that I could glue together later.

All of a sudden, literally from nowhere, a stiff wind hit. It nearly knocked me off my feet, shrieking and carrying red dust from Utah that quickly obscured the basin. Within minutes, I was in the middle of a gale-force windstorm with almost zero visibility.

I couldn't believe that conditions could change that fast. Apparently that dark cloud was bringing some really nasty weather.

I quickly managed to get my big pack onto my back and head down the trial with a sense of urgency. The wind was bitter cold, cutting right through me. I could barely stay on my feet, and it had gotten noticeably darker. It was soon spitting snow, making everything slick.

I felt like an idiot. What kind of outdoorsman would ignore all the obvious signs? This was the kind of ignorance that led to people reading about your demise in the paper and commenting on how stupid you were.

The Darwin Award, they called it. Climber goes alone, tells no one, sees signs of a major storm all over the place, ignores signs—oh, and a Bigfoot...throw that in for good measure.

Now I was in a full-on blizzard, and it had been only 20 minutes ago I was blissfully eating a PBJ on a rock in the sunshine. I grew up in the mountains of Colorado, and I knew how fast conditions could change, yet here I was, stumbling down a rocky trail that would lead me in a couple of hours to the safety of my car, if only I could see where to go.

The visibility got worse and worse, and I could no longer even make out the trail. Where the heck was I? I needed to stop and set up my tent and hunker down before I got totally lost. But the winds were so vicious I wasn't even sure I could get my tent up. And what if it snowed several feet? My little tent would be totally buried.

Oh man, I was now worried sick. How the hell did I get in this predicament?

Now I could barely make out something dark nearby, and it didn't look like a rock or tree—it was the old cabin! I had somehow managed to stumble up to the old cabin!

The door was laying there on the ground, so I just went on in. It was weird, having the winds drop off. As soon as I was inside, there was no wind buffeting me around, and I could kind of gather my senses.

The cabin was old and decaying and musty, with one corner kind of collapsing, but it had stood there for at least a hundred years, so I guessed I could safely spend a night there without worry.

It was now almost dark from the storm, so I pulled out my headlamp and proceeded to organize my camp around me before it got totally dark. My down sleeping bag would probably get me through the night, and I'd just have to pray I didn't get snowed in.

I spread my pad out and shook out the bag, hoping there weren't any other critters in the cabin that would want to sleep with me.

I sat there for awhile, then decided to make some dinner, freeze-dried beef stew. The winds howled on as I slowly ate. After that, there was nothing to do but hunker down in my bag and try to stay warm.

It was only about six or seven in the evening, but it was dark. I was soon fast asleep, the wind raging outside. I had climbed a big mountain, so I was tired. Plus the lack of oxygen at that altitude makes you want to sleep.

It must've been about midnight when I woke. The winds were unbelievable. I went to college in Boulder, and I once was in 70 m.p.h. winds there, and these seemed even higher. The whole cabin shook, and I wondered if the old structure would make it through. I can't begin to describe the fury of the winds, it was as scary as it could get.

I got out of my bag and shined my light out the door. The snow had stopped, which was good. I might be able to get out as soon as daylight came. It looked like there was only about three or four inches on the ground.

It was then that I noticed a faint odor like a cross between something dead and a ripe garbage can. It was inside the cabin. I hadn't noticed it before—had I just missed it from all the craziness of trying to get settled and survive? It was definitely not there before, I decided, as I have a sensitive nose and would have smelled it, no matter what. It was puzzling.

I crawled back into my bag, wanting to preserve the warmth. I lay there, trying to go back to sleep, but that odor had me puzzled. What was it? Was it just the smell of the old cabin?

Maybe, but in these winds, any smells should be over in Silverton or beyond by now, as the cabin was getting lots of ventilation. Something didn't feel right.

I finally drifted back off, warm in my bag, still tired.

I have no idea how long I slept before I woke again. The odor was now stronger, and a sixth sense told me to lay completely still. There was something in the cabin with me, something alive and smelly. I didn't dare turn on my light or even move. I was terrified. What if it were the creature from last night?

I lay there, frozen in fear. I finally heard something over in the corner opposite me, which must have been loud to be heard over the wind. I listened.

It was someone snoring! Oh my God, there was someone in here, and they were really big to make that kind of snore.

And now I needed to pee, but didn't dare move, and this only added to my misery.

I lay there as the wind howled and the night slowly wore on, wondering if I were dreaming. Finally, I gave up, slipped out of my bag, peed in the corner of the building, then crawled back into bed.

After crawling back into my bag, I could see two red eyes shining in the darkness. They had nothing to reflect off of, they were shining with their own energy. I was again terrified.

I had an overwhelming urge to sleep, and I tried to fight it, but couldn't. I drifted off. Whatever it was, if it wanted to harm me, there wasn't much I could do about it, and it seemed like it was just seeking shelter, like me.

I thought about this later, and I really did fight that sleeping feeling. I wanted to stay awake with all my might, as I was afraid of dying in there, but I just couldn't. It was almost like I'd been drugged.

I woke at dawn, and the creature was gone. The winds had stopped completely, and a soft snow was falling. I quickly gathered my gear and headed down the hill. The trail was mostly covered with snow, but it wasn't hard to make out the way, just go down.

A few hours later, I found my car. It had about six inches of snow on it, and it was now snowing harder. I cleaned off the windshield, prayed it would start, which it did, then cranked the heater, and headed out.

I barely made it to the highway, sliding and skidding, as the forest service road wasn't plowed. It was August, for God's sake.

I drove into Silverton and got a motel room. No way was I going to try to get over Red Mountain Pass in a snowstorm, I hated driving it when it was dry. I think I slept all day, as I don't really remember much, except luxuriating in the warmth and security.

I did wake several times in terror, thinking I could hear loud snoring.

I knew what was making the sound up in that cabin, because I saw its footprints in the snow as I headed out. At least 20 inches long and with five toes, what I'd call a Bigfoot.

[3] The Intruder

. . . .

One of the best things about my job, other than working in beautiful places, is the people I get to meet. Flyfishermen are the best. They like getting out because of their love of the outdoors, and the fishing is just an excuse.

It used to be that my clients were exclusively male, but that's changed over the years. I'm glad for it, as the women I've guided seem to be even more in tune with nature. What this means for me are quieter trips and better food, as they always want to pitch in and help cook. The gals also can tell some good stories, like the following.

My name is Cammie, and all my life I've been afraid of becoming a bag lady. In a way, it came true. I guess when your greatest fears come true, you learn to deal with them. Maybe you subconsciously test yourself by making them come true, but it sure didn't feel like I had much to do with it.

I had a good job and a nice house when the economy tanked. A lot of hard-working people lost everything, and I was no exception. Without my job, I could no longer make my house payments. It was a long downward spiral, one I tried my best to avoid, but after awhile I had nothing left, I mean nothing.

My health wasn't even so great, as the stress of it all really did a number on me. I developed arthritis in my back, which made things harder.

Before I knew what had happened, I was homeless. I'm kind of solitary by nature, so I've never had tons of friends, and the few I had weren't able to help. I was too proud to ask anyway.

My family was gone, and it was just me. It's a helpless, hopeless, sinking feeling, believe me. All I had was an old car and a tent and some camping gear. I was grateful to have even that.

Because I couldn't afford gas, I knew I had to stay close to town, where I could get water and a bit of food. I was on food stamps at that point, the only assistance I could get, and it's really hard to job hunt when you're camping out. In any case, a job didn't appear to be forthcoming, not that there seemed to be any, anyway.

So, where could I camp, be close to town, and yet be safe? Fortunately, I was living at that time in a little town, which made things easier.

It had a beautiful eight-hole golf course by the river, so I headed for that, as it was right on the edge of town, yet close to everything.

I set up my little tent out behind some bushes and established that as my camp. I didn't dare park my car where anyone would notice, so I asked permission to park it at the truck stop a few blocks down, and they said that was fine.

So, I would sneak in and out, getting my car when I needed to go anywhere, but basically staying on the edge of the golf course, my tent hidden in the bushes.

This course was beautiful, with huge cottonwoods and lots of lush greenery, and I actually felt very peaceful there, in spite of my situation.

Keep in mind that I had always owned a beautiful home—well, owned along with the bank, I guess, or I would still have it. But my house was always very nice, and I had nice stuff. All gone now.

But the golf course made life bearable, it was so pretty. Of course, it was spring, so we'd see what winter brought, if I were still there. Hopefully I would have something going by then.

It took awhile, but I gradually established a sort of routine. I'd use the river water to wash and kept clean, also doing my laundry there. Nobody came down there, so it was very private, just me and the ducks and a few geese.

I didn't dare drink the river water, but the golf course had little water stands everywhere for the golfers to get drinks, so I did fine with that, filling gallon jugs when I needed water for coffee and cooking. It was pretty nice, water fountains and benches and lots of beautiful plants.

In the evenings, after all the golfers left, it was like having my own private gardens, as if I were rich. And since it was a small town, there never were many people there. It really lifted my spirits sometimes, even though I had no place to go when it rained or it was too hot.

I had been there a couple of weeks and was beginning to relax a bit, no longer fearing being discovered, when

I decided to go exploring one evening. I walked down the golf paths to the end of the course, which banked up against the river, where an old railroad bridge crossed.

I enjoyed watching the trains go by, so I started hanging out there some to relieve the boredom. I would pretend I was getting on Amtrak and heading back to my hometown, where everything was good like it used to be. But then I would get depressed, so I had to stop playing that game.

One evening as I sat watching the sunset over the river, I noticed the evening light was shining off something metal across a field filled with weeds as high as I was. I didn't want to walk over there to see what it was, so I went up on one of the golf course hills, where I could see out a bit.

I could see the metal roof and top third of what appeared to be an old abandoned brick building, completely surrounded by tall weeds.

The town I was in was gradually losing the economic battle, just as I had done, and a once proud railroad and mining town was falling into disrepair and abandonment, desperately trying to attract tourists, but with none of the amenities that tourists want.

It was becoming a very poor town, and I knew I wasn't the only homeless person there.

From my vantage point, I could see a path through the weeds to the edge of the golf course, and I suspected someone had holed up at the abandoned building, just as I had done in my tent down the course a ways.

I decided I should become more careful about not being seen in the evenings, when I tended to be more casual.

This took some of the peacefulness from my life, knowing someone else probably lived there, as the path was well-worn.

I even decided I probably shouldn't be coming down there to watch the trains, so I stopped doing that. It had been my only connection with the outside world, so I missed it.

After a month or so, I knew I would survive, but I also knew this had to be a temporary situation. There must be something I could do to improve my lot.

I began looking for a job again, anything, even going door to door at the local businesses, but found nothing. I was beginning to feel a deep despair and had even contemplated ending my life.

But the beauty of the golf course kept me going somehow, even though I was despondent. I checked out books from the library, but that got old—I needed more variety. I tried my hand at writing, but I didn't have a knack for it.

I had spent my entire life as a professional photographer, and now I didn't even have a camera. I needed something to do, some way to make money and have meaning in my life.

Life was getting harder and harder mentally, as I had no idea where to turn, and I didn't want to spend the rest of my life in a tent.

It was now late spring and the days were getting hot, which made things even more difficult. I now spent more time down at the river, dipping in the water to stay cool.

At least it cooled down at night, and I slept well in the peacefulness of the cricket concerts. And I loved hearing the whistle of the trains as they came through town in the night.

I believe it was about late-May, and I was feeling especially desperate, seeing how quickly time was passing and how little progress I'd made towards finding work. One consolation was that all the work of camping was actually helping my back, limbering me up.

I knew at that point that I needed to get to a larger town, but I had no money for gas or a place to stay. It was a Catch 22, I was stuck. I was depressed, and I decided to go down to the river to watch the birds and cheer myself up.

I'm a very quiet person and don't like to announce my presence, especially in the situation I was in, so I very quietly made my way through the willows towards the river bank.

Something was different this time. A sixth sense seemed to kick in, and I stayed in the willows a bit, assessing the situation. I could hear something, but I couldn't put my finger on what it was.

As I stood there in the shadows, I thought I was finally beginning to go nuts, something I'd heard that homeless people do. I couldn't believe what I was seeing.

There, on my little river beach, were two young bears, dancing and playing in the water, wrestling with each other and having a great time, getting soaking wet.

You have to understand that the little town I was in had no bears for many many miles around, the nearest bear habitat was probably a good 60 miles away. It was too hot here for bears, with nothing for them to eat. It was flat country, not mountainous. To see not just bears, but two young bears playing in the water, was beyond belief.

But something wasn't quite right. The creatures were covered in fur from head to toe and played on all fours, but they also stood upright, and their faces weren't bear-like, they were more like humans. And they held sticks and things with their hands, something bears can't do.

The realization slowly sank in, and I began to feel a cold terror. These were not bears. What were they?

I had to get out of there. It was all too much. I fought daily to maintain what little sanity I had by trying to create some security around me through daily habits and remembrances of a former life, and now my entire world was being shaken by seeing something that I didn't know existed, and right in my back yard. What were they?

I turned and quietly snuck back to my camp area, where I basically collapsed. I was scared I was losing my mind. My normal frame of reference was gone.

I slept all afternoon under a big cottonwood back in the bushes, and when I woke, I felt better. Maybe it had been a dream. Maybe I had hallucinated it all.

But I knew better, I knew what I had seen, and deep in my heart, I knew what it was. I have a friend who lives in the Gold Country in northern California, and she's told me many stories of Bigfoot.

These were Bigfoot children, right here, in my refuge. And where there are children, there are adults. I didn't have a safe place to get away from them.

I could hear Amtrak going by, whistling at the crossings in town, and I wanted nothing more than to be on that train, safe and going somewhere, to a life of meaning, a home. I wanted it so badly that it actually made my stomach hurt until I thought I would throw up.

I would have to move camp, I decided, but to where? About the only other places around town were in the open, with no privacy or places to hide. People would see me and know I was camping, leading to who knows what?

I was desperate. There was no one left to ask for help, even asking the two local churches earlier had led nowhere. Everyone was broke or trying to keep their own heads above water.

I knew I couldn't spend another night there, not with Bigfoot around. And then it dawned on me that the path I'd seen, the old abandoned building, that was their home.

They probably caught ducks and fish from the river for food, maybe killing an occasional deer and eating cattails and other riparian plants. I was the intruder, not them.

But I had nowhere to go. To make things worse, a flock of buzzards was circling the golf course. I suspected they were migrating north, but it seemed a portent to me, especially when dusk came and about 30 of them roosted in a nearby dead cottonwood.

I normally love all kinds of birds, am fascinated by them, even buzzards with their graceful ways of floating on the air currents, but I was in a dark frame of mind and pictured them picking my bones clean after the Bigfoot got finished.

I finally grabbed my sleeping bag and headed for the truck stop, where I slept in my car, feeling safe and secure under the neon lights and amid the constant hum of truck engines.

I'm sure in retrospect that the Bigfoot family knew I was there all along. I was smack in their territory and had been foolish to assume I was the only one around.

They had probably spied on me, and come to think of it, I do recall the first few nights there feeling very scared, like someone was watching me, so much so that the hair on my neck had stood up. But that subsided, and soon all felt well.

They probably had no problem with my presence, but I was unable to accept theirs. There was no way I could return to my camp, at least not to sleep, and I was beside myself trying to figure out what to do.

I was stiff and sore from sleeping in my car, and I had to get the rest of my gear, so I headed back to the golf course. I skirted the greens, as there were a couple of players, and I didn't want to be seen.

What happened next changed my life, even though it was a very simple thing.

Lying at my feet, obviously wounded, was some kind of hawk. It was fierce and wouldn't let me near it, lunging at me with its sharp beak, but it badly needed help. It was unable to fly, and I found three large feathers nearby that appeared to belong to it.

I took off my jacket. No way was I going to let this bird die without at least trying to help. I would catch it and take it to the truck stop and see if anyone knew who could help.

The bird was about the size of a red-tail hawk. It was becoming tired and not quite as nervous of me, as if it were accepting its fate. I quickly threw my jacket over its head, then grabbed it, wrapping it so it couldn't scratch or bite at me, its head covered just enough so it could breathe.

It went totally limp, a survival mechanism some wild animals have to avoid advertising their vulnerability in bad situations.

I then ran directly across the greens, carrying it, where a man with a golf cart saw me and asked what was wrong.

He offered to help, so I jumped in his cart and we drove quickly to his car. Before long, the two of us were at the vet, who took a look at it and said it needed to go to the bird rehab place.

We were soon our way to the next town, a good hour away, where the bird rehab place had agreed to take the hawk.

Complete strangers, united in our common concern for a wild bird, riding along in the car, talking, while the bird was now safe in a dog carrier in the back seat. The guy's name was Dave, and he was a real gem.

The bird was a rare Harlan red-tail, a hawk that was part of the red-tail family but had no red coloring. The woman who took care of the birds examined it, then bemoaned that we hadn't been able to get the missing feathers.

It had lost them in a fight or something, maybe with a buzzard, but if we had them, she could glue them back on and the bird would be fine. Instead, she would have to call other rehabbers to see who possibly had anything that would work. The feathers were critical flight feathers, rendering the bird helpless without them.

Dave and I drove back to the golf course, where we searched for the feathers, to no avail. He then bought me lunch at the nice golf course restaurant.

I was hesitant to even hang out with him, wondering if it was obvious that my hair needed washing and my clothes were washed in river water.

He didn't seem to notice, or if he did, he didn't care. We talked about birds and places we'd hiked and camped and it was two hours before we left the restaurant.

I was wanting to look again for the missing feathers, and Dave wanted to go with me to see if we could find them, so off we went. We asked around, thinking maybe some golfer had found them. No such luck.

Now came what I'd been dreading, the time when Dave would ask where I lived and all that, and of course, he did. I decided to be totally honest with him. I had nothing to lose.

I told him to follow me, and to his surprise, I showed him my little camp in the bushes. He looked very surprised, but took it in stride and was very kind.

But when I found the three feathers stuck in the edge of my pack, I felt waves of fear and peace go through me, both at the same time.

The only ones who could've done this were the Bigfoot family, they were the only ones who knew where I lived, and they had obviously seen me rescue the bird.

Next to my pack were two little round river pebbles, polished perfectly smooth and colored with what appeared to be some kind of plant pigment. I knew it was a gift from the youngsters. I felt humbled after being so afraid of them. They meant me no harm.

Dave was really happy we had the feathers. I told him someone must have found them and known I had rescued the hawk, which was true, though I neglected to tell him that the someone was from a different species.

He insisted that we take the feathers to the rehab place immediately, so off we went. We delivered the feathers, and when we got back, it was nearly dark, so he bought me a room in the local B&B, refusing to take no for an answer.

I can't tell you how luxurious a real bed and shower felt, as well as the security of being indoors. I cried when he dropped me off there.

He was back the next day, and we went and got my gear from the golf course bushes. He had a small apartment he was going to let me stay in until I could find a job.

I swear, I felt like I had met my own guardian angel, and I was so very grateful. He was a local, the son of a prominent rancher, and he had made his living as a contractor, investing in properties, and was fairly well off.

When we got my gear, I felt that old feeling that I was being watched, but there was no malevolence. Dave felt it too, remarking on it later. He said I had been very brave to camp there.

After getting settled in my new apartment, I returned to the golf course with a gift. I walked to the beginning of the path to the old building, and there I left a big package of groceries, stuff I'd bought with the last of my food stamps—a huge ham, some fruit, crackers and cheese, and a bag of sugar, and candy bars for the children.

When I left it, I knew I was being watched, and I sat for a moment as Amtrak went by, wondering what my future held, but knowing I would never again fear the darkness.

One week later, I had the privilege of releasing the hawk at the same place I'd found it while the rehab people and a reporter took photos. Dave was there, also, and I felt the presence of others, but couldn't say anything. I knew the Bigfoot family was watching.

I keep the two pebbles in my pocket all the time, a reminder that no matter how bad things get, there are others who care. And I now have a job working in bird rehab. Dave is a board member of the new non-profit he and I started, as well as a donor, and I'm the director.

Once a week, I take a big package of food down to my Bigfoot family, though I no longer have to use food stamps to buy it. They always leave me gifts in return—rocks, sticks, and sometimes even a small bird feather.

[4] Bigfoot Potluck

Here's another story told by a woman on one of my trips, Susie. She and her husband, Cal, had a great time fishing, as did their black lab, Zady, who spent all day every day splashing in the river and retrieving sticks. Zady was actually more of a gray lab at that point, as she was pretty old. I thought she would scare the fish away, but the couple ended up catching more than most people, so I think she chased the fish to them.

Susie and Cal loved that dog, and I've often wondered what would have become of Zady if she hadn't happened to be in the same place and time as that most elusive and rare of creatures, the Bigfoot. Zady was very lucky, as was the Bigfoot.

Have you ever seen a big San Rafael Swell tank? That's what they call potholes out there, cause they're so huge, they're more like big tanks. What and where's the San Rafael Swell? It's a place in central Utah that will blow your mind.

My husband, Cal, and I have spent a lot of time out there because it's such fascinating wild country. We always used to take our black Lab, Zady, with us, until she got too old to go.

But let me tell you about a time when Zady had the adventure of her life. I think we did, too. It was about ten years ago, when we were all younger and not wiser and did some pretty interesting things. Seems we've slowed down a bit since then. OK, we've slowed down a lot since then.

Cal and I had planned this trip for months. It was our spring vacation. We get two weeks off in the spring during spring break at our school, one of the nice benefits of being teachers.

We would always go out to Utah and hike and camp, and it was usually a great time to be out there, as the weather was typically mild then.

We were in great shape, and we had gotten into canyoneering, which is more than just exploring canyons, it involves getting in and out (hopefully) of canyons you can't just hike through, but have to rappel, hike, climb, and sometimes even swim. It can be really grueling and a bit scary at times, but really isn't life-threatening unless you screw up.

People do screw up, though, like the guy who was hiking one easy canyon and took a wrong turn and ended up dead. He slipped down a pour over, thinking he could keep going, and below him was another bigger one he couldn't get down. At that point, he couldn't get up, either. That was a sad story, for sure.

We're pretty thorough on our route finding, but this one time we really screwed up, in spite of having studied

Google Earth, topo maps, and reading a local guide book. What we found wasn't in any guide book.

Some of the canyons of the Swell are really just too narrow, you can't even get through them. They either squeeze down too much or the rappels are too high. But most of them are just fun challenges, if you know what you're doing and are in good shape. Oh, and if it isn't raining up higher and you don't have flash floods. Those are the real killers.

And like they say, there's no substitute for feet on the ground, so sometimes all your research isn't the same as being there, you find that things aren't what they seem. That's what happened to us.

The canyons of the Swell all erode down from about 7,000 feet, where the Swell tops out, to about 4,000, where the San Rafael Desert meets them and they turn into washes, eventually working their way through the flatter desert to the Colorado River.

I've been on those lower washes, and they're usually wide and low-banked, and you would never guess what wild places the water in them has been—when they have water, that is.

They're usually completely dry until a good rain pushes down from the upper Swell, and then it all comes at once. There's one wash out there north of the San Rafael River that's wider in places than a small river, but it's bone dry.

But you can see debris a good 100 feet up on either side of its banks. That wide wash was carrying a lot of water to overflow its banks that much.

So, you can imagine what those slot canyons in the Swell can be like in a rainstorm. You don't want to find out, that's for sure.

Cal and Zady and I got out there in late spring, and you could tell it had rained not too long before, because there was some standing water in the small potholes where we parked our car by the head of the canyon.

That meant we might be swimming. That water can be icy cold in the spring. You can get hypothermia real quick in some of those big tanks if you stay in too long.

We had pretty good-sized day packs with plenty of water, as you really don't want to drink the Swell water, as it carries a lot of selenium, and there are also wild burros and cattle out there, which can mean giardia.

We also had food and flashlights and matches and everything you need to survive, as well as climbing gear for rappeling and any possible climbs. We wanted to be able to climb around any pour overs if we couldn't get down them.

We felt we were prepared for about anything, we even had a climbing harness for Zady. And of course we both carried small inner tubes and a portable battery-operated pump to blow them up. These were in case we came to some big deep tanks.

So, early morning, we were up, and off we went. The plan was to canyoneer our way down this somewhat obscure and unnamed little canyon that looked like it became a slot and then come out at the bottom. We would then hike back up around on top to get back to the car.

You can hike the sickrock and avoid the slots to get back. That was the plan.

Zady loves to go with us, and she's a good dog in every way. She minds pretty well, and she loves to swim, being a lab. She was barking her fool head off all the way down, playing in the water in the little potholes along the way and chasing the sticks Cal would throw.

Before long, the canyon narrowed into a delightful place, nice and shady, and we even found a few petroglyphs. We sat down and had an early lunch, enchanted by the canyon, our real lives and worries far away.

A pair of ravens floated down to check us out, and I threw them bites from my sandwich, but Zady got them instead. She had her own gourmet doggie hiking bars, but she wanted our boring sandwiches. Typical Zady.

After a bit, we continued on, and the canyon narrowed, just as we suspected it would. Zady led the way, her excitement contagious. We were having a great time, and it didn't look like anyone else had been here recently, nary a track.

The canyon quickly narrowed, and we were soon hiking along the sandy bottom of a slot canyon. There was debris a good 20 feet above out heads, indicating the depth the flash floods got. It was spooky.

We knew we weren't in any flood danger, as the sky was clear as far as we could see, and spring is a good time to hike as you usually don't get afternoon thunderstorms.

But slots are a bit spooky, and sometimes I get a bit claustrophobic. This one was quickly narrowing and soon we had to turn sideways to get through. We had considered that we might have to turn around and hike back up the canyon if it got too narrow, we just didn't know what it would do. The topo map indicated it stayed fairly passable, but maps can be a bit off, depending on the scale.

Zady led on, tail wagging. Now the canyon was almost too tight to get through, and I was beginning to think we would have to turn back.

Now Zady was whining, and we could see that she had gotten far enough ahead of us to where the canyon narrowed too much for passage. She was stuck and couldn't turn around and was panicking instead of walking backwards out of it.

Cal and I quickly ran to her, as we didn't want her to go any further if she did manage to get unstuck, but we were too late. She popped on through the tight spot, and next thing we knew, we heard a loud splash.

Our beautiful day now quickly became a nightmare. Zady had slipped through the tight spot and managed to fall off a pour over into a tank, from the sounds of it, and we had no way to get to her to bring her back up. I felt panicked.

Cal quickly assessed the situation, looking up the canyon walls to see if there were any way he could climb up and over, but the canyon was a good 50 feet deep at this point.

There was absolutely no way to scale the walls, and we just didn't have enough hardware to get us up there, even though we had a rope that long.

I could hear Zady swimming and splashing around, and it sounded like there was no place to get out of the water. Some of these tanks have steep sides and no place to push off to get out. We'd rescued her a couple of times on hikes when she would jump in and not be able to get out.

She had learned to not just jump in unless she had permission, which is pretty good for a water dog. No big deal when you're there where you can just reach in and grab her collar, but now we couldn't get to her. And as cold as the water was, she would soon be hypothermic.

I felt sick and had no idea what to do. I tried to squeeze through the slot, as I'm smaller than Cal, but no way, and we didn't have a lot of time to help her.

Now Zady was whining in the most pitiful way, and I knew she was scared and getting cold and tired. How long could she keep swimming?

Cal was still trying to find a way up and over when suddenly Zady's voice changed from a pitiful whine to a growl, then to the bark of a very frightened dog.

Now she was yelping, as if something were harming her, and I could just picture a cougar attacking her, as the Swell is home to a number of them.

I started crying, thinking of what she was going through and how helpless we were.

Then, all of a sudden, she was back with us. She looked shocked, and I'm sure we did, too. Something had lifted her up and pushed her back through the slot. There was no way she could have jumped back through it.

Sweet Mary, how did this happen? It was a miracle.

Zady was soaked and shivering, and I wrapped my jacket around her and held her to me, comforting both her and myself.

Cal was at the slot, calling out, "Who's there? Thank you. Are you OK? Are you stuck?" He got down on his knees and tried to see through the narrow space.

There was no answer. Zady was now settling down, but every time she would look at the slot, she would start shivering again. I watched her and knew this was from fear, not just from being cold.

She was scared stiff of whatever had helped her get out. This was too weird, because whatever it was, it had to be human to lift her, it had to have hands.

Just then, the most heart-wrenching moaning came from below the slot. It made me feel like I was hearing the voice of something from long ago, from some kind of primal forest that no longer existed, from some creature almost extinct that maybe the early Indians in this region had moved into cliff dwellings to hide from.

"Oh my God," Cal said, "There's something stuck down there." I noted he didn't say "somebody."

"What can we do?" I asked.

"All I know is to backtrack and see if we can get out of the canyon and up above. Maybe we can help that way."

We started back up the canyon. I put Zady on her leash, no way was I going to have any more worries. She didn't act like she was going anywhere anyway, she was totally deflated and still shaking. Since she was now pretty much dry, I deduced she was still scared to death.

The way she carried her tail between her legs and kept trying to get me to carry her confirmed it. I haven't carried her since she was a pup, she's too big.

We felt a sense of urgency. If something or someone was stuck down there, they also would be in the water, just like Zady, and hypothermia is the number one killer of hikers and adventurers, even in the desert.

Before long, we found a place where we could climb out and were soon above the canyon on the slickrock above. Picture a big kidney-shaped mountain about 60 miles long and 30 wide, with deep canyons cutting through it, and you'll have the Swell.

We were now on the slickrock above the slot canyon, where we could walk alongside it and look down into it.

We soon figured we were near the area where we'd been standing just before, the place where Zady got stuck.

We walked a bit further, and Cal then inched over to the edge on his belly so he could see down into the depths.

Our estimate was good, he was directly above what appeared to be a deep tank, right below a pour over about 10 feet tall. That must be where Zady slipped down into the water, landing with the splash we'd heard.

"Anybody down there?" Cal yelled. We were a good fifty feet above the canyon bottom. He shined our flashlight down into the depths, but it was too far down and too dark.

Now we heard the moaning again. We were directly above it. What could we do?

Cal took out our rope, tied one end to a nearby juniper, tied a foot Prussic onto the other end, then threw it down, yelling, "Put your foot into the end and we'll pull you up!"

There was no response. He looked down and could see the end of the rope dangling about 15 feet above the tank. It was almost long enough, but not quite.

"OK," I said out loud, talking mostly to myself, "there has to be a bit of a lip above that tank, as it took a moment before we heard Zady slide down into the water. If we can go back down into the canyon and get the rope down through that slot, whoever is down there can climb it back up to that lip and at least get out of the cold water. The rope might reach them if we can then get back up here and drop it back down."

We all ran back along the canyon, dropping back into it and rushing down to the slot. Cal took the rope and tossed it through the slot, but it didn't seem to go anywhere.

He started yelling again, "Are you still there? Are you OK? We're trying to get a rope down to you. Answer if you're OK."

No sound, but then we heard splashing and I knew whatever it was still was alive and in there. We had to help it. It had saved Zady, now we had to return the favor.

"There has to be a way," I said out loud, thinking again, but unable to come up with anything. Then suddenly, I knew.

I found a long stick that had been carried down in the flash flood debris, a stick about 12 feet long. I tied one end of the rope to the stick, then pushed the stick through the slot.

My hunch was right, the slot wasn't that long, and we could hear the stick fall into the tank below.

Would whoever or whatever see what we were trying to do and climb out? Was there even a big enough space above the tank to stand on?

"On belay!" Cal cried, having wrapped the rope around his waist, hoping the person below would start climbing.

"Holy crap!" he immediately called out. "Susie, hurry quick, I'm losing it." He began wrapping it around a rock.

I grabbed the rope and held on for dear life. Whoever it was, was very heavy, but we managed to keep the rope from slipping until it went slack. I knew they were now standing on the other side of the narrow slot. Now what?

Now we heard a new sound, a low humph, and it was very close. Zady's hackles stood up, but she didn't growl.

Now we would run back up above and figure out how to get them out. At least now they weren't in the water, and maybe now the rope would reach.

Cal tugged on the rope until it was released and he could pulled it back through the slot.

"We'll be back," he yelled, "Don't go away."

We climbed back out of the canyon and were soon above the tank again. Now, Cal tied one end of the rope to a big juniper tree.

He tied Zady's harness to the other end, presumably to give the person something to hold on to as we pulled them out. He then tossed it over the edge.

"On belay!" he called. There was no response. Had the rope gone where we wanted? He crawled again to the edge to peer over, and yes, we were right above the tank.

He pulled the rope up and tossed it in again. Maybe they hadn't been able to reach it. This time, it was immediately taut.

Cal started trying to pull the rope up, but it didn't budge. Was it stuck? He looked over the edge again, but this time, he quickly jumped up.

"Get away!" he yelled at me, grabbing me by the arm and pulling me and Zady away from the rope. I thought maybe it was tangling or something.

I had no idea what was going on. He kept pulling me away, and we were soon a good 50 feet from the edge, standing behind a big juniper.

Just then, what emerged from that canyon made me rub my eyes in disbelief.

A thin creature stood there, covered head to toe in white hair, except around its eyes and mouth, where the skin was dark. It was at least seven feet tall, and reminded me of a cross between a gorilla and a human, the body being gorilla-like and the face being human.

Zady whimpered and had her hackles up and tried again to get me to hold her. I sank to the ground in disbelief and shock. Cal just stood there.

The creature had climbed up the rope like a monkey, really fast. It stood there in the bright sunlight for a moment as if in disbelief, looking at us with its big eyes. There was no white in its eyes, I remember that. It was soaked and shivering.

It looked like it would collapse, but it slowly turned and walked away, down the face of the Swell.

I wondered how it had ended up in a tank deep in a slot canyon in the Swell, though I've since heard of other Bigfoot encounters in the upper forests of that region, over near Richfield. Maybe it had slipped and fallen in, trying to get a drink, coming up from below.

After it had walked a ways, it stopped and turned back, and I'll never forget what it then did. It spoke to us, saying something in a voice that carried like thunder, but that was gentle and subdued and even a bit sad.

I don't know what the words meant, but I do know what the meaning was—it was thanking us.

Cal saluted it. It turned and left, and we never saw it again.

[5] Pumped up at
the Pump Jack

This is one of the stories I've heard that wasn't told around a campfire. Bud, the storyteller, was a guy I met while sitting in front of the town library under some big trees, enjoying the sunny day and reading a newspaper.

Bud sat down on the bench opposite me and started reading his paper, and before long, we were talking. He was from southern New Mexico and was in town for a week or so visiting his daughter. He was looking for things to entertain himself with while she worked, so we ended up doing some four-wheeling together, and that's when he told this story. He was a real character and I really enjoyed hanging out with him.

I'm Bud, and me and my brother Charlie had something really strange happen to us a few years back. I still to this day have no idea why it happened.

At the time, we both worked for a big oil company that has a gazillion pump jacks, and our job was to maintain them. We were based out of Carlsbad, New Mexico, and if you've ever flown over that country, you'll see that we had a big job, as there are literally thousands of pump jacks out there. Of course, we weren't the only guys doing this, but we did get stretched pretty thin sometimes.

Charlie and me didn't work together unless it was something that required a second hand. We mostly just drove around from pump to pump, checking to make sure everything was working.

We had a routine and it was usually pretty predictable. Nothing much ever happened, which was how we liked it.

We both lived in Carlsbad, though Charlie's wife lived up the road in Artesia, but that's another story. We shared a little house out on the road to that little state park with all the desert displays, which I thought was a waste of space, since everything out here is desert, but that's also another story.

I kind of liked my job, as it put me out in the country most of the time, far away from people, which was good for me and good for the human race.

I used to tend to drink when I was unhappy, so I needed something to keep me happy, and being out away from everyone's problems did just that, kept me happy.

I loved driving all over the place and still being home at night, unlike the trucker job I had a few years before, which was why I got divorced, yet another story. As you can see, my life is full of stories, some good, some bad.

I haven't decided yet if this story is good or bad, maybe a bit of both. The bad is the crazy scary dreams I still have, but the good is that it woke me up a little, started me to realizing that there are things out there we don't have a clue about.

Now you may laugh, but this story is about a Bigfoot. Yeah, I know, everybody says I'm nuts, crazy, to consider a Bigfoot living in southern New Mexico, in the heat and cholla and mesquite and ocotillo. What the heck would they eat? And where do they get their water?

An animal that big would need plenty of both, and that part of the country don't have much of either.

Maybe they drink oil, I don't know. There's plenty of it out there in what's called the Permian Basin, that's for sure.

That country was once a big swamp, and the Guadalupe Mountains, way over in Texas, which you could barely see from our house, the geologists say that was once a big coral reef.

Ancient swamps and oceans and coral reefs mean one thing—gas and oil. I guess that's two things, isn't it? Those two things are what provided me and Larry with good country-fried steaks down at the Carlsbad Diner every Friday night after work.

Anyway, on with the story. It was winter, which is the only time that damn country's even inhabitable, and then the weather can be downright nice, even though the countryside's still as ugly as ever.

I mean, people come from up north to winter around there, so I guess we have something going for us, even though there isn't much for scenery, and that damn refinery up in Artesia sure smells things up when the wind's just right.

You wake up to this sickeningly sweet odor, just drifting down over the hills, and it's disgusting, but you get used to it. The local businesses say it's the smell of money, but they don't seem to realize that the only reason the tourists go down there is for the mild weather and to see the caverns, other than that, nobody would ever go down to that ugly town.

But the local businesses think it's someplace special. Give them one good recession when the tourists stay home, and they'll lose some of that arrogance.

OK, so where was I? Oh yes, it was winter, which is probably the only time of year a Bigfoot could be in those parts with that big fur coat on.

Maybe someone could start a Bigfoot barbershop and do OK, more of the big fellows would come visit in the winter, could supplement the tourism, add something to see because the scenery sure ain't worth nothin', or did I already mention that?

Boy, I sure do get sidetracked. Anyway, it was winter and maybe about 60 degrees outside, and I had just met Charlie for lunch.

He had a route that kind of intersected mine, and we usually managed to hit each other about lunch time, so we typically had lunch down at Pump #234, which is a bit up on higher ground, if you could call anywhere around there high ground, it's all so flat. But it's on a hill, and we could see a bit out, so we'd just sit there and eat lunch together and talk about whatever, but not the scenery.

Not until this particular day, anyway, when Charlie was sitting there eating his sandwich. Mine was identical, since it had been my day to fix our lunches, usually baloney, as we ate a lot of that and that could explain a few things, but here I go again, getting off road and stuck.

I had finished my lunch and was taking a nap, dreaming about fishing in Montana, no sound but the occasional thump of the pump jack when it reached apogee and perigee on its course.

All of a sudden, Charlie reached over and kicked the bottom of my boot, waking me up.

I could see he was kind of squinting, having just had cataract surgery and not being used to his new eyes yet, looking way out at something, and I figured this had something to do with why he woke me up, so I asked him what he was looking at and he said he didn't know, but there was some kind of thing coming up the road and it looked to be on legs, not wheels, but it wasn't a cow or anything like it, yet it was too big to be human and was all brown, head to toe.

I turned to see what he saw, but my eyes aren't as good, since I haven't yet had cataract surgery, as I'm waiting to see how Charlie does with it. All I could make out was a dot. But I could see that it was moving along at a good clip, coming right our way.

Charlie now sat up straight and said he didn't have a good feeling about this.

I asked if it could be a mad bull or something, looking for some humans to destroy because of our baloney sandwiches (I'm not really sure what's actually in baloney), and Charlie just ignored me.

Pretty soon he was on his feet and telling me we should maybe get out of there, because whatever it was, it was big and it was fast, and it was coming straight our way.

I asked him if maybe we weren't seeing what they called an apparition, and he answered that apparitions don't kick up dust.

It had only been a minute, but when I looked again, I could see why he was concerned. This thing was big, it was running really fast on two legs, and it looked to be a grizzly bear or something like it.

I thought maybe I was still dreaming, in Montana, cause we sure as hell don't have grizzly bears in southern New Mexico.

"I'm getting the hell out of here. Let's go," Charlie said, heading for his pickup.

"I'm with you, but it's coming up the road, we'll run right into it, which looks like a bad thing to do. What the hell is it, anyway?" I asked.

"Let's follow this old drill road out. It crosses the hill and comes down the back and meets up with the main road back there. That way we can avoid it." Charlie replied.

We took off, and I can assure you we wasted no time, Charlie following me up the old washed-out drill road. We were both fit to be tied, another way of saying scared crapless.

What in the heck? Roswell wasn't that far away, maybe they had called down some weird experimental alien with their UFO stuff.

We bounced those trucks and popped gears all the way up that hill, and when we got to the top, I turned around to see what was going on. Charlie was right behind me, and not far behind him was one of the scariest sights I've ever seen.

Damn, he was big. Then I thought, this thing is really hairy. He looked to be about seven feet tall, all hair, and with massive shoulders. The hair on his head blended with the hair on his body.

I thought maybe it was some idiot in a suit, but no human could ever run that fast, so I decided it was a creature I had never seen before. It would take a complete lack of brains to dress up in a monkey suit, as in this part of the country everyone would shoot first and ask later. Everybody has a pickup with long guns in the rear window.

Looking back, I can say that its shape was basically that of an upright human, but there were definitely some gorilla-like characteristics as well.

It had a conical head with what appeared to be a crest. It was incredibly muscular, and I was especially struck by the sheer size of its biceps and the thickness of its body. Like a gorilla, I could see no neck.

Charlie honked his horn while yelling for me to get going, and I headed down the other side as fast as I could go. The road was even worse on that side, all washed out and rutted, and I nearly got high-centered more than once, but managed to gun my way out of trouble.

All of a sudden I heard Charlie honking again madly, and I slowed down and looked back.

He was stuck, rocking his truck back and forth, gunning it, but stuck like a jackrabbit in New Mexico gumbo.

He jumped out and ran up and jumped into my cab, yelling "Go! Go! Go!" totally panicked.

The weird creature was now beside Charlie's stuck truck, pausing for a moment before continuing to come after us, and I gunned it as hard as I could.

We bounced and careened down the hill, and when I got to the main road, the truck actually slammed down onto it a foot or two, nearly knocking all my teeth out, but I didn't even pause, I just gunned it some more and kept going. It's a wonder I hadn't popped a tire or broken an axle.

Charlie was watching behind us the whole time, and he later told me that this thing had been close enough to grab the tailgate, but I had hit a bump just then, throwing it back. I couldn't believe its speed, it was just hard to process how fast it could run.

Now on the main road, I was going about 50 and yet managed to hold it together, skidding around corners and about scaring myself to death with my exceptional driving skills. We hadn't even reached pavement yet.

When we did finally get to the highway, I looked over at Charlie, and he was white as a sheet and shedding a few tears. I figured they were tears of joy, but he told me he was still scared crapless and asking me what it was. He then asked what to do about his truck.

As mad as that thing was, I didn't figure there would be any truck left to worry about, but I didn't tell him that. What worried me more was trying to explain to the boss what had happened to his truck. No way would anyone ever believe us, they'd just start looking for the whiskey bottle under the seat.

"I could sure use a stiff drink," I said.

"I'm worried that thing will follow us home," Charlie replied, even though by now we were on the pavement and doing at least 75. "Let's go on up to LuAnn's in Artesia and spend the night."

We headed on up to Artesia, where Charlie's wife Lu-Ann was happy to see us and didn't act a bit surprised. "I knew you boys would come see me for my birthday," she smiled. I knew Charlie had forgotten all about it.

We took LuAnn out for country-fried steak, then I left and ran into the store and got her some flowers and a nice card, which I gave to Charlie to give her.

He stuck a little cash in it and pretended he'd known all along and that was the reason for our visit. Neither of us mentioned one word about the Bigfoot or whatever it was. We were both shell-shocked and barely said a word to anyone.

I went to bed in the guest room, hardly sleeping a wink, wondering about what I'd seen and why.

When I saw Charlie the next morning, I knew he hadn't slept any either, and I assumed it was for the same reason, though I could've been wrong.

He told me he was calling in and quitting, and his excuse was that he'd got drunk and left the pickup out there and just didn't want to work there no more, that was his story, and I was to stick with it if the boss asked me questions.

I drove on back to the house and managed to make it out to work only a bit late, in spite of everything. I just went to work as usual, but with one difference—I now carried a long rifle in my window rack, and it was loaded.

At lunch, I decided to go up and take a look at that truck, but it was gone. Apparently the boss had come and got it first thing. I never did hear if it had any damage or not, and the boss never mentioned anything to me about nothing.

Maybe he'd seen the beast too, and just wanted to forget about it. I had my suspicions, as he started drinking on the job, and I was soon promoted to his job.

That was fine by me, as it meant I wouldn't be out in the field much. I would just have to try and learn how to deal with being happy some other way, and humanity would have to get used to having me around.

And of course, Charlie never came home, except to get his stuff. He got a job with LuAnn at the refinery, leaving me to batch all by myself.

But things change, and one day I met a cute ranger from that state desert park up the road. We're getting married in a few weeks, so I won't be living alone much longer.

I even went up there and visited her museum, and it's really pretty nice, has a lot of nice desert stuff. One of these days I'll ask her if she's ever considered adding a Bigfoot to the collection.

I never did figure out what happened that day, but I finally quit trying. I think maybe that fellow was migrating through, and he just wanted some baloney sandwich for lunch. One thing I do know, he wasn't there for the scenery.

[6] The Windigo of Grand Mesa

I heard this story told next to a Wyoming campfire, a ways from my home stomping grounds of Colorado. I was there working for a few weeks with a friend who has a guiding business and needed some temporary help, as one of his guides had fallen off a ladder while working on the roof of his house, breaking his ankle. So I went up to help.

The storyteller, Jamie, was very soft-spoken, and I had no idea he taught at a university until he told his story. Nor did I know he'd had a life-long interest in cryptid creatures, which includes Bigfoot. If I had known, I think we would have had some interesting talks, but the trip ended the next morning, so it wasn't meant to be. But his story was quite the tale.

My name is Jamie, and my sister's name is Jennie. Those are not our real names, of course, and you'll understand why after I tell our story.

I'm a professor at a university, and this story could end my career if certain people knew, especially since I'm a psychology prof, so I don't tell it often.

It wouldn't impact my sis as much, as she and her husband own an RV park in a beautiful resort town in Colorado, which ironically isn't all that far from where this story took place. I will say she doesn't go out in the forest there, and her kids don't go out without their dad.

Jen and I were both young. I was 10 and she was 12 when this event happened. It's been many years ago, but it left an indelible mark on us both and altered our lives. In fact, I became a student of cryptid creatures and human psychology to try and explain what happened.

I'm not even sure where to start. Sometimes retelling events brings us closure, helps us understand ourselves and what happened and why.

It all started when our parents decided we needed to go to summer church camp. Our mom and dad weren't particularly religious, but we did all go to church occasionally. I think they thought it was something they needed to do to raise us to be good people, since they'd been raised that way.

Our church, just a standard protestant church, owned a beautiful camp in the foothills of Grand Mesa, a huge wild mesa in Western Colorado that some claim is the largest mesa in the world.

I'm not even sure how many miles long it is, but it stretches at least 50 or 60 miles in length. It's pocketed with lakes of all sizes, and most are inaccessible except by horseback or hiking.

I you want to get into the backcountry there, you'd better plan on carrying a machete, as a lot of it is just thickets

of scrub oak until you get up higher in the aspen and ever-
greens.

It's beautiful country, but it's wild, and all those lakes
breed a special form of mosquito that seems to be able to
bite through anything.

Anyway, one nice summer day, Jen and I were informed
that we were going to a week's worth of summer church
camp on the edge of the Grand Mesa.

Neither of us were too thrilled with this. We are both
kind of the more academic types, not real sociable, and we
would have preferred staying home and reading books to
what we considered a week-long indoctrination camp.

We begged and pleaded with our folks, but to no avail.
They were determined to make us more sociable and do
their duties in the religion department. Like I said, neither
were very religious, and maybe they figured this was their
way of insuring we'd all go to heaven if it did happen to be
real.

Jen and I called it fire insurance camp. We thought that
was really funny, but our parents didn't.

So, we packed our stuff, and off we went on the church
bus with about 20 other reluctant kids to get a week's
worth of who knows what. We had no idea what one even
did at church camp.

Well, the first thing they did was separate us into boys'
and girls' dorms. That meant I would see Jen only at meals
pretty much from there out, as the boys and girls had separate curriculums.

I had hoped at least to have Jen to commiserate with while there, since I didn't know anyone else except casually from the few church meetings we'd been to. Divide and conquer seemed to be their strategy.

The first night there was really weird. I was immediately homesick, but that wasn't what made it weird. My bed was under one of the crank-open windows that ran along the ends of the long building that made up the boys' dorm. I could open and close it at will, and since I like fresh air, the first thing I did was open it.

What made the night weird was hearing strange sounds that seemed to come from the edge of the big clearing that skirted the church camp, from deep in the forested thickets.

I lay there and listened. It was my first night there, and I felt I had accurately assessed the place, it was weird. And the more I listened, the more I thought that—and I got scared.

The sound I was hearing wasn't at all like the coyotes I'd heard on family camping trips. It was an awful shrieking and screaming demon type sound.

I was uncomfortable and thought that there was something in those woods, something that howled like it was dying. It actually sounded like a wild man out there, and I had the feeling that there was something wrong, terribly wrong.

I just wanted to go home. At one point, one of the other boys came over to my bunk so he could listen and it really freaked him out. He told me he was never going close to those woods, no matter what activities they had planned.

It wasn't long before all the boys in the dorm were by the windows listening. I don't think any of us got any sleep, and our overactive imaginations didn't help matters any.

This howling went on all night, and it seemed to have a deep resonance to it that carried for a long ways. It would carry on the wind and get louder, then fade away into the night. We would think it was gone, then it would start in again. We were all about to pee our pants.

Another thing of interest was that our camp counsellor, the person supposed to be staying with us in the dorm as a supervisor and chaperone, seemed to be having some kind of an affair.

That first night there, I'll call this guy Bob, he told us he liked to go to the chapel late at night and pray when everything was quiet and he could meditate.

Bob snuck out at about 9 p.m., leaving us to our own devices, after a short lecture on how he knew he could trust us to act like adults until he returned in a few hours and not mention his absence to anyone. It was just between us and him and the bedpost.

What he didn't know was that we could see the chapel from one of the windows, and one of the guys spied him going in there with the counsellor from the girls' dorm, who I'll call Jill.

Seems like Bob and Jill had a lot of meditating to do, cause Bob didn't come back until about 4 a.m., after the action with the weird noises had finally stopped. But he probably didn't mind, as he was having plenty of action of his own in the chapel.

After the howling finally stopped, we all managed to go to sleep. I woke up when Bob come in and then dozed back off.

The next day at breakfast I told Jen about everything and asked if anyone in her dorm had heard anything. The girls' dorm was on the other side of ours, away from the woods, so they hadn't, but they were all soon aware of what had gone on, and some voiced their desire to go home that very day.

And of course they were now aware of the fact that their chaperone had disappeared during part of the night, which left everyone even more scared, as they didn't like being alone.

After breakfast, we were all herded into the chapel, where we listened to the camp leader give a short sermon. I don't remember much of it, just stuff about how grateful we should all be that we could come to such a special and wonderful camp and stuff like that.

We were then herded right back into the main hall, which had now been cleared of the breakfast stuff, where we were assigned "units" and given an overview of what our daily activities would be.

Each unit was made of four people, and this group would be our "family" until the end of camp. We would do everything together, including dishes and KP duty. It was beginning to remind me of what I'd heard about the military, an entity I never planned on learning about first-hand.

A week isn't long to an adult, but to a kid, it can be a long time, and I figured the way things were going it would be more like forever.

And to think my parents were paying for all this. Being an innocent kid, it didn't occur to me until years later that what they were actually paying for was a week off without the kids around.

Jen and I managed to talk to each other long enough for her to inform me that she was going to get sick. I didn't even have time to ask her how she knew that, as she was soon gone, off with her unit to play "scriptural badminton," whatever that was.

She had it all planned out, a way to bail out and go home. She told the camp nurse she was sick, so she ended up in the nurse's room with a thermometer stuck under her tongue. She sat there and held her breath, hoping to somehow make her temperature go up.

Another camp had seen a case of rheumatic fever, though Jen didn't know this, and her plan almost worked, as the nurse was more paranoid than usual.

Jen got her temp up by a whole degree, which earned her a day off resting in her dorm. If she didn't get better, she might be sent home, she was told, to which she protested, but the nurse insisted. My sis has always been adept at gaming the system.

I suffered through our first day while Jen lounged around in her dorm, reading books. The rest of us spent most of the day outside—after all, it was a summer camp, and all of us eyed the nearby woods with concern after last night's strangeness.

Nobody made any effort to go after a baseball that someone hit deep into the undercover. We just declared it lost and got another.

Jen didn't show up for dinner, and I had no idea what was going on until asking my camp leader, and he informed me that she was sick.

Knowing what she was probably up to, I snuck some dinner to her via another girl. I also found out where her bunk was, so I could talk to her after dark through the window.

That night, as I was about to go out and talk to Jen, the howling started up again, though this time it seemed closer. I lost my nerve and couldn't go out, especially after Willy, my next-door bunkmate, started telling us creepy stories about the Windigo.

Willy's family was originally from Alberta, and Canada supposedly has this wild beast called the Windigo that lures you to it by sounding like a crying woman or baby.

Willy at first seemed to delight in scaring the pants off us all, but as the howls got closer, he got really quiet and asked me to close my window. He must have believed his own stories.

Someone suggested we go get one of the camp leaders, but nobody had the nerve to leave the building. Of course, our chaperone was long gone to his nightly "meditation" in the chapel.

To make things worse, the wind picked up and was soon whipping around the building, but we could still hear the strange beast with its long, doleful wailing.

I shivered and closed my window, but curiosity got the better of me, and I reopened it. We could now hear what sounded like a siren in the distance, though there wasn't a town nearby.

It sounded just like a fire siren, and it would get louder and louder, then it would recede into the night and stop, then after awhile, start again. It sounded far away.

This really got everyone going, and now we could hear what sounded like someone chopping wood deep in the forest. By now it was near midnight, and we were all exhausted from being up the previous night, but no one could tear themselves away.

It was almost like we were afraid that if we gave in and dropped off to sleep we might sleep right through our own demise. That's how scared we were, and we all vowed to call our parents in the morning, have them come and get us, and never come back.

If nothing else, these night events were bonding us, and someone suggested it was the camp leaders doing this intentionally to scare us so we wouldn't sneak around after dark. If so, it was working.

We all worried about Bob and Jill and hoped they survived their walk home from what we were now calling the Chapel of Love.

You can imagine how I felt when just then something tapped on my window. Just about every boy in the dorm jumped and ran away, a couple even screamed like girls. I was too scared to even move.

I then heard Jen's voice: "Jamie, come outside, I think I'm leaving tomorrow. I need to talk to you."

Willie yelled out, "My God, girl, get inside fast, your life is in danger, run!"

I quickly unlocked the dorm door, and Jen came in, bumping into things in the dark. "What's going on?" she asked, "Why am I in danger?"

Just then the howling began again, but now almost at the window. It was deep, had a strong resonance to it, and it undulated, seeming to push through the walls of the building.

Jen gasped and grabbed onto me, her knees collapsing. Now all the boys were huddled nearby, some shivering, one even crying.

Willy took command, I guess cause he was the expert on weird beasts, and he cranked the window closed while ordering someone else to make sure the doors were locked and another to check that all the windows were cranked tight.

We were all terrified as the howling intensified, along with the wind, battering the sides of the dorm. Willy commanded everyone to prop chairs and bunks against the doors in case the thing tried to break in.

After a mad scramble, we all kind of huddled together, sitting in a tight circle in the center of the room in the dark. For a bit, the winds died down and all was quiet. Now a strange moaning sound started up.

Suddenly, something crashed onto the roof, something heavy. Willy yelled, "It's on the roof!"—just to make sure everyone was properly scared, I guess.

More crashes followed that, and we soon decided it was throwing rocks or logs or something up there. I was wishing I had my 12 gage shotgun, the one I used for target practice back home.

Now all was quiet again. We were considering what to do next, when we heard a thumping noise on the side of the building, like something was whacking it to test its strength. The boy who had been crying earlier started up again.

Now the rocks started again, landing on the roof. When we went outside the next day, we saw dozens of rocks on the roof, ranging from baseball size to the size of a microwave.

Willie had strategically placed someone to watch the chapel so we could assess when Bob and Jill left it and what to do. We had tried to figure out some way to warn them, but hadn't come up with anything yet.

Sure enough, around 4 a.m., the door opened, and they emerged into the darkness.

Willie quickly opened a window and started yelling at them to go back into the chapel, but they apparently couldn't make out what he was saying over the wind, as they continued up the path to the dorms, hand in hand.

Now we didn't know what to do. To say we were scared speechless was an understatement. None of us would have ventured outside under any circumstance, yet someone needed to warn the couple of their impending doom.

The pair was on the opposite side of the building from where we'd last heard the Windigo or whatever it was, which again began moaning, confirming it hadn't yet seen them.

Bob and Jill were talking fairly loudly for a couple sneaking around in the night, and we deduced that the

Chapel of Love was serving double duty as the Lord's Ale House. The moaning stopped, and we knew the beast had now heard them. What could we do?

The boy at the window watching the chapel was the first to actually see the creature. He began shaking and yelling uncontrollably, trying to warn the couple, and Willie and Jen and I ran to the window.

What we saw made me want to throw up from fear. I somehow went into a tunnel vision kind of moment. It's hard to describe, but all I saw or thought of was this huge thing. I have never felt more alive and was totally focused on it.

It was big and had a human shape with glowing eyes. It was too dark to make out any color, and it had massive shoulders. It seemed to be wearing a hoodie jacket, as it had no neck, the shoulders just melted up into its head.

If you were to put it at a typical doorway, its shoulders would have extended a full foot beyond the door's width. It had a dark face with dark skin visable through its hair.

Now it appeared to be stalking the couple, and they were totally unaware of it. It was only about 20 feet behind them, hiding in the bushes along the walk, following along. They stopped for a late night kiss, embracing as the beast swayed behind them.

"We have to do something, we can't just stand here and watch them get killed," Jen said.

"What can we do?" I asked.

Jen didn't even answer, but started for the door, calling us words I had no idea she even knew, words that alluded to our lack of courage. She rushed out the door screaming and yelling, straight down the path towards the unsuspecting couple.

I couldn't stand and watch my only sister be eaten by a Bigfoot or whatever it was, so I ran out the door behind her, also screaming and yelling like a banshee from hell.

I guess we inspired the others, because a few of them ran out after us, making a commotion that ended up waking the entire camp.

We ran straight towards Bob and Jill, who must have been totally shocked. Jen grabbed Jill by the arm, yelling to get inside, their lives were in danger, and we hustled them back into the dorm.

Just then, the beast screamed, and that was all it took. Everyone ran as fast as they could, no one wanting to be last.

We slammed the door and locked it, and Willie went to the window to watch, but could see nothing.

Just then we heard a loud whoosh, and something hit against the side of the dorm. We later found a huge six-foot branch that had been torn off a nearby tree.

Bob called the camp leader on his cell phone, and the sheriff was soon there. It was now almost dawn, so everyone pretty much just hung tight while the sheriff and his deputy drove around the perimeter of the camp with their searchlight. They didn't see a thing.

At dawn, tracks were found all over the place. The rocks on top of the building were discovered, and it wasn't long before everyone boarded the buses to return home. The camp was closed.

Come to find out, this wasn't the first visit for this particular church camp visitor. It hadn't acted as bold before, and the camp personnel had managed to keep everything under wraps. But no longer.

Last I heard, the camp was closed and eventually sold to a corporate mogul who was going to set up a hunting camp for his wealthy clients. I bet that went over real well with the Windigo.

It took Jen and I years to really come to grips with this episode, to process it and be rid of our night fears, as much as one can, anyway.

We've stayed in touch with Willy, who now owns a restaurant in the city and refuses to this day to go camping. I can't say I blame him any, as I also won't go out after dark into the woods, and rarely even during the day. One encounter is enough for me.

And I don't think there was one kid on those buses that regretted church camp ending early.

[7] Just One Little Drink

This great story was told around a campfire deep in the heart of Bigfoot country, at a gathering of some friends in western Washington. The fellow who told it is a friend of a friend, and I had never met him until that particular night.

It was different, hearing about a Bigfoot near Holbrook, in northern Arizona, out in the desert. But I do know that Holbrook is only an hour or so from the forests around Show Low, as well as Flagstaff, and there have been plenty of Bigfoot reports from both areas. So maybe it wasn't as unlikely to hear of a Bigfoot out in that desert as one might think.

This isn't a first-hand story, but rather one my grandpa told me. He's as honest as the day is long, so I believe it really happened. My dad said he believes it, too. I think it took place sometime in the 1970s.

My grandpa was a cattle rancher. He worked very hard all his life on a place he inherited from his dad, although he added greatly to it, buying acreage and building lots of fence and cattle sheds. He ended up owning over 5,000 acres when all was said and done.

That may sound like a lot of land, but when you need a couple of hundred acres to support one cow, you can see that the more of that kind of land you own, the poorer you are.

My dad inherited the ranch, but he hated ranching, had trouble paying the tax bills, and my mom wanted to live in town, so he ended up selling it for a song and dance. Otherwise, I might've become a rancher myself instead of running a tire shop.

I probably would have hated ranching eventually, as it's nothing but hard work, according to my dad, who started the shop I now own, two states away from where he grew up on the ranch.

So, go back to sometime in the 1970s and picture my grandpa, in his forties, tall and a bit too thin, wearing his old beat-up Stetson and run-down-at-the-heel Tony Llama cowboy boots, a blue plaid button-down shirt and faded Levis, smoking an Old Gold cigarette while driving an old beater Chevy pickup he bought used from some old guy at the livestock auction over in Holbrook—on his way to fix fence or repair a windmill. His blue merle Aussie Cattle Dog, Joey, was always at his side, day and night.

If you've ever been to Holbrook, Arizona, you'll know why my dad hated ranching. That country is full of salts and poisons that nothing much can grow on. It's some of the most barren country on the planet, not far from the Petrified Forest.

It's hard to believe my grandpa made a go of ranching there, and I sometimes wonder how well-off he might have been if he'd had decent conditions to work with, as he was a smart and hard-working man.

The key to raising cattle there was having water, as it's just barren desert. With water to drink, the cattle seem to wander and find enough to eat, though one has to supplement their feed and then move them up into higher country in the summer to get them out of the heat.

My grandpa had some leased land over by Flagstaff where he would truck his cattle for the summer, fattening them up on tall mountain grasses.

But back to his ranch, which was called the Broken Stirrup Ranch. My grandpa spent a lot of his time running around checking on cattle and fixing fence, going from windmill to windmill, making sure they were working OK, as a cow or steer could die really fast without water.

These big ole windmills sucked water up from a deep aquifer, pumping it into big stock tanks, and it wasn't bad water. Of course, other animals would come and drink from the tanks, usually at night, especially antelope.

But one time, my grandpa had a visitor that wasn't like anything the Broken Stirrup had ever seen before or probably since. I think he almost left the ranch over this, and he had been through many hard times, so that tells you something.

My grandma was normally the kind of person who saw the world as she wanted to, not as it really was, and would avoid anything out of the ordinary. Yet she stood by this story her whole life.

In fact, she eventually started going out with Grandpa while this was all happening to be sure he wasn't alone. My grandma was a real homebody, so she must've been really worried to do this.

So, one day my grandpa is out checking this particular windmill, and he notices there aren't any cattle around, not a one, and Joey is whining his little head off.

Now, this is unusual, as the cattle always come to the tank to hang around in the heat of the day, and they get in your way when you're there trying to check on things.

This worried my grandpa, so he started driving around the area looking for them. He would just take off cross-country, no roads, and you can do that out in those badlands, as long as you watch where you're going.

He got up on a rise, and no cattle were to be seen anywhere. He was especially worried because it was about time to start calving.

He finally spotted them clear over at the fence along the highway, all huddled up together as if they'd stampeded and couldn't get any further than the fence, but sure would like to leave the country.

He checked on them, and they all seemed fine, but he was puzzled. They seemed glad to see him, and since he was supplementing their grazing at that time with hay, he had some bales in his pickup, and they followed him on back over to the windmill, hungry and thirsty.

They seemed really leery, but they did finally come up and drink, but they were really spooked. He noted all this, trying to figure out what had happened.

Something had scared them, he knew that, and the way Joey was whining was odd, he never did that unless something was wrong. Grandpa threw the hay out, hung around awhile to watch them, and finally left after everything seemed back to normal again.

He noticed in his rear-view mirror that as soon as he left, they scattered, so he drove back. They hadn't begun to finish the hay, and when they saw him there, they came back and started eating again.

This really puzzled him. They were still scared, but his presence seemed to make them less fearful.

So, he stuck around while they finished the hay and drank, checking the windmill and all that while waiting. It was then he noticed some weird prints in the mud around the tank, really weird prints like nothing he'd ever seen, really big and wide and having five toes, like a human.

Joey was whining again, all upset, wanting to get back in the truck. Joey always rode in the cab with Grandpa, but since the doors were closed, he jumped into the bed and tried to hide. He never did ride in the bed, he was a dog of luxury, unlike other cowdogs.

Grandpa tried to track the prints, but they just disappeared when they crossed a nearby slickrock outcropping. Joey wouldn't get out of the truck bed, he always went everywhere with Grandpa, but no way would he help him track.

This made Grandpa worry, too. Something was way wrong. He was afraid to try to look for the tracks any further.

This all really spooked my grandpa, and he now understood why the cattle were so nervous. He got out his high-powered binoculars from the pickup and glassed the countryside all around, seeing nothing, and he could see for a long ways in that open country.

Now my grandpa could smell something foul. It about made him gag. Just then, a small herd of about eight antelope came running hell-bent up to where the cattle were kind of picking at the hay, still nervous.

This caused the cattle to take off again, and the antelope stayed with them. This made my grandpa think the antelope were more afraid of something out there than they were of him and were seeking safety with the cattle.

He stayed there for about an hour, watching, but saw nothing. Finally, he left, having things to do, but he later went back with more hay and enticed the cattle back to the tanks. They were all thirsty and drank for a long time. The antelope were still with them.

That evening before going home for the day, my grandpa checked on the livestock again. They seemed happy, lolling around the tank, chewing their cuds. Whatever it was, it was apparently gone.

Next morning, he was back out there bright and early, as he hadn't slept well, worrying about those tracks. Sure enough, no cattle. The entire scenario was repeated, and he finally got the cattle back over to the tank and settled down. The antelope had moved on.

This time he counted them to make sure they were all there, which they were. He was worried that all this stress was bound to make them start calving early, and he didn't want that.

What was he to do? Something was scaring his cattle, and what if it actually harmed one of them? This worried him.

He had lived in Oregon for a couple of years as a kid when his dad had worked for the lumber mills there before moving to Arizona, and he knew well the stories of Bigfoot. That's exactly what the tracks had to be, nothing else worked.

But how in heck could there be a Bigfoot on a dry Arizona ranch? How did it get there, and what did it eat? That latter question is what worried him the most.

He went home mid-day, which he rarely did, and my grandma knew something had to be wrong. He told her what was going on, and she freaked.

She made sure he had his loaded rifle with him, and as I said earlier, she eventually started riding in the truck with him until this was all over.

They talked about what to do, and my grandma was pretty firm about my grandpa having to somehow get rid of whatever it was, as it was disturbing the cattle.

So, Gramma hopped in the pickup with Gramps and Joey, and off they went. She had her Polaroid camera and wanted to see the tracks—which she did, and that really freaked her out because it confirmed that Grandpa wasn't seeing things.

I still have those old photos, but they're so faded you can't make much out.

Grandpa knew that another sleepless night was on its way, so he decided he might as well spend it out watching the cattle. Gramma didn't like this one bit, but Gramps did it anyway, spending the night at the tank, sleeping in his truck with one eye open and a rifle in his hands, Joey curled up by his side.

Nothing happened, morning came, and all was fine, so he went home and got some real sleep, he and Gramma returning in the afternoon. Everything was still A-OK.

Now, Gramma wasn't the kind of person to just stand by and let her livelihood be compromised, so she did something that Grandpa was at first upset about, but later decided was a good idea—she talked to the neighbors, what there were, anyway, out in the middle of nowhere.

She then called their friends at the Bobwire Ranch over by Flagstaff and asked if they'd had any weird going-ons. Come to find out, they had, which I think surprised her.

They, too, had seen strange things, but they had a regular crew of hired men and had put out night guards, and eventually whatever it was left—but not until it had killed and partly eaten a yearling calf.

They had actually seen it in the dark and shot at it, and this is when it finally got the message and left. She thanked them for sending it her way and invited everyone over to help stand night guard, which they said they would be happy to do if she and Grandpa needed help, but not until after calving. She said she would get back to them after talking to Gramps.

Gramps was now very very concerned after hearing the thing had eaten a calf. He was beside himself, he couldn't stay up all night guarding and also run a cattle ranch, he would die of exhaustion. He was already sleep-deprived and grouchy. What to do?

All he could think of was to go back out and check on everyone. This time, he drove on past his gate to the stretch by the highway where the cattle always ended up. He might as well go with the flow.

Sure enough, there they were, bellowing and milling around as if something had just stampeded them.

All of a sudden Joey just went ballistic, barking at something on the crest of the hill. And that's when Grandpa saw it for the first time. It wasn't at all what he'd been looking for, as it wasn't black, but a reddish-tan color that blended right into the hills.

Maybe this thing wasn't a newcomer at all, but part of a line that had adapted to the desert, seeing how well it blended in and all.

This really bothered him, so much so that he immediately jumped out of his truck and started shooting at it, even though it was a good half-mile away. He hadn't shot that rifle for a good five years or more.

It ran like the wind before he got a chance to get out his binoculars and take a good look, but in all honesty, he was more interested in shooting it. He could look at it when it was a goner.

But he had an unsettled feeling, even though he couldn't see it very well, it looked too much like a human. Bigger and faster than any human, but still very much like a human.

It was then he noticed he'd left his truck right in the highway and a semi was coming from up the road, so he jumped in and managed to get it to the side of the road before disaster hit.

This made him feel like a fool, which led to his cussing the Bigfoot to no end, wishing it were back in hell where he figured it belonged.

He hadn't seen it well enough to be traumatized by it, but his time would come, even though he had no inkling of this at the time.

There was no way he was going to get the cattle back over to the tank, so he turned around and went home. He needed help.

So, Gramma again called the boys at the Bobwire.

They weren't sure what to do, as they were in the thick of the start of calving season, but offered again to come help when things slowed down.

Gramma was now expressing her interest in coming up there and giving them a piece of her mind when one of the guys had an idea. Why didn't Grandpa just get a camp trailer and stay out with the cattle until things settled down?

The Bobwire had good success with someone staying with their cattle, and things had mellowed out a bunch after they did that.

Grandpa wasn't too happy about this, as he didn't have the money for a camp trailer, but Gramma soon had it all figured out. She called the Fitzgerald-Garcia Sheep Ranch and borrowed a sheep wagon. All they had to do was go get it.

Grandpa was now frustrated with Gramma, he didn't want anything to do with sheep, he was a cattle rancher. He didn't even want to sleep in a wagon that was called a sheep wagon.

But Gramma prevailed and the wagon was soon set up next to the tank, all outfitted with coffee and supplies.

Grandpa would spend his first night there that very night. Gramma worried about him, but he convinced her nothing could happen while he was locked up in a tin can.

He was about to find out how wrong he was.

That night, he camped out by the tank. He kind of enjoyed it, building a big fire and sitting there watching the stars and reminiscing about his youth when he ran cattle for the Bobwire, which is where he cut his teeth in the business.

He then got to wondering what his life would've been like if he'd done something different, like maybe open a tire shop.

The cattle were happy to have him there, and they all hung around close by, as if seeking his security and guard. He could hear them lowing contentedly, and before he knew it, he was fast asleep, his head on a small log and his feet to the fire, which he had banked with a couple of large logs from his autumn forays into the mountains.

His plan was to sleep in the sheep wagon, but he never got that far, he was just too tired.

Joey was of course with him, a good dog, sleeping at his master's feet. He adored Grandpa, and they were inseparable pals.

Sometime in the middle of the night, Joey woke Grandpa, growling in a voice he had never heard him use before.

The cattle were restless, and even though it took Grandpa a minute to remember where he was, he lost no time.

His trusty rifle was at his side, and he quickly grabbed it up and got himself and Joey into the sheep wagon, where he could assess things with some safety.

Now he could hear the cattle making all kinds of noise, and he knew the creature had to be nearby. He stepped out of the wagon and fired a few shots into the air, which was all it took to stampede the cattle.

There they went again, off to the fence line by the highway. Nothing he could do about that, except follow to make sure they were OK. He was getting damned tired of all this and just wanted a good night's sleep, nothing more.

He was collecting a few things to take with him, a thermos of coffee and a jacket, when he felt something slam against the side of the sheep wagon so hard he thought maybe he'd left the truck out of gear and it had rolled into it.

He looked out the side window, but there was no truck there. Whatever it was had hit the wagon so hard it had actually tipped it a bit, which made Grandpa pretty uncomfortable.

Joey was barking madly again, but after a few moments he disappeared under Grandpa's sleeping bag on the bunk, hiding, quiet as a mouse.

This was totally unlike the bold dog who had once chased a black bear from camp up in the San Francisco Mountains.

Grandpa stood there for a bit, scared stiff, with Joey bravely under the covers, wondering what next. After awhile, he figured he needed to get out and go check on the cattle.

As he finally worked up the courage to get out of the wagon and into his truck, he heard the most blood-curdling scream imaginable from the distance. It made his blood run cold, and he never forgot it.

Joey, who apparently hadn't planned on going anywhere except under the covers, came running out from the wagon and jumped into the truck, shaking like a leaf, trying to actually get under the truck seat.

Grandpa felt sorry for him and put his coat over him so he'd feel safe, then hightailed it out of there, going back over to the highway to check on everyone.

By now, Grandpa was totally exhausted and scared to death. It seemed to him that the Bigfoot had left for now and the cattle were OK, so he drove on home, leaving the cattle to fret in their corner by the fence.

Of course, when he related everything to Gramma, she was soon on the phone again to the Bobwire boys, making them feel more than guilty for running that damn monster over their way. They promised they would send two guys over to help that night.

They were good on their promise, sending two cowboys over who stayed in the sheep wagon and took turns guarding the cattle. Grandpa finally got some sleep.

They reported all was well and the cattle had started their calving that very night. Seems like they had waited for everything to settle down to have their babies, which cattle have been known to do.

With the help of the Bobwire boys, Grandpa was finally able to get everything under control, and the Bigfoot seemed to know what was up, because it stayed away the entire time they were around, which ended up being several weeks.

With calving finally over, Grandpa moved into the sheep wagon for a couple of weeks, watching the calves at night and making sure everything was OK.

The Bigfoot was still gone, but Grandpa decided to haul the cattle a bit early to his mountain land, as it was shaping up to be a nice mild spring, and he didn't want to risk losing any calves to the beast. He somehow knew in his heart it would be back.

The Bobwire boys came down and helped him load everyone up in the cattle trucks, and they were soon on their way up to the mountains.

Every year after that, Grandpa hired them to come down from Flag and help out. I guess he realized there was a limit to what one man could do.

Fast forward to mid-summer, the cattle were happily grazing in the high country, and Grandpa was out at the tank, working on windmill maintenance. All was well until he noticed Joey has his hackles up. The dog then jumped into the truck, shaking.

Grandpa looked where Joey had been looking and saw the creature over in the shade of an old abandoned shack.

He could now see it clearly. The top of its head was cone shaped, and it had long hair on its head that came down to its shoulders on both sides, covering part of its face. It seemed to not have any neck, but the head just kind of melted into the shoulders.

Its body hair was shorter and very unkempt looking. He could make out a closed mouth, a flat nose, a heavy brow line, and the eyes were all dark, with no white showing.

Its face was like an aborigine. After seeing it, Grandpa said he could never shoot one, they were too human.

At first Grandpa was scared to death, and he started to make his way over to the truck and his rifle, but he then noticed that the creature seemed to be having trouble standing up, as if it were dizzy or something.

It then dawned on Grandpa that all it wanted was water, just a little drink of water.

So he got into the truck and drove off a ways, then just sat there watching. I can say he had more nerve than I would've had to stick around, but he was always a curious kind of guy.

Sure enough, it was dying of thirst. It barely managed to drag itself over to the tank, where it then actually climbed into the water, drinking while sitting in the tank.

That tank was several feet deep, and Grandpa said the Bigfoot must've been at least eight feet tall to stick up as much as it did when sitting there.

After it seemed to get enough to drink, it just sat there looking at Gramps, and Gramps said it just seemed to look right into his soul. It scared him to death, and yet he knew then it wouldn't hurt him.

It seemed to be able to tell Gramps' thoughts, at least that's how he felt. It really creeped him out, so he threw his lunch out the window for it and drove away. It was pretty scrawny looking.

The very next day Gramps had to go to Flag for some salt and supplies, and he came upon a road-killed deer and had a light-bulb moment.

He had a small winch in the back of his pickup for pulling bales of hay into the bed, and he stopped and hooked that dead deer up and hauled it into the back of his pickup.

He said people were giving him strange looks as they drove by, so at one point he pointed to the deer and rubbed his tummy, which gave him a good laugh, knowing those travelers would think he was going to have that dead road-killed deer for dinner. He was always a character.

This was an idea along the lines of how he always came up with things, spur of the moment and pretty crazy, but they usually worked out.

So he took that deer back to the tank and dropped it off back where the tracks had led into the area, hoping it would give the Bigfoot something to eat.

He checked a few days later, and sure enough, the deer was gone. He didn't see the creature any more after that, but he knew it had come into the tank area a few more times for water, as he saw some fresh tracks.

He told my dad he thought it had left the area for good as soon as it had the strength, because nobody ever saw it again, and it never bothered any livestock.

Until he passed away, Gramps always told people about how he saved a Bigfoot's life after he first tried to shoot it.

He always got a kick out of their reactions, as he knew they all thought he was a liar, but then he would pull out a photo he took of it while it was sitting in that tank, as he had happened to have Gramma's old Polaroid camera with him.

Their tune would change to shock and amazement, then they would accuse him of staging it with a guy in a suit.

This provided endless entertainment for Gramps through the years.

Too bad he never did anything to try and save that photo, cause it eventually faded out and was gone. I personally think it would have done a lot for the science of Bigfoot, as well as making him a rich man.

[8] Sarah's Bigfoot Boat Float

• •

I met the teller of the next tale, appropriately enough, at her pizza bar. A couple of buddies and I were on a road trip to check out some new fishing country up in northern Washington.

I asked about the Bigfoot reference in the name of the root-beer float I had just ordered (Sarah's Bigfoot Boat Float), and the following story was my answer.

It started when I stepped out of the bar and nearly stepped on a badger.

No, I hadn't been drinking, and I doubt if it had, either, unless it was drinking river water. It was one a.m., and my sister and I had just closed everything down.

Our little pizza bar here caters to the college crowd, so it's sometimes a lot of fun, sometimes not, depending on what part of the semester it is.

Ironically, finals week is when we do our most business. The week after finals is usually good, too. I guess the same kids who blow it by procrastinating at the bar come back to drown their sorrows.

But generally the kids are nice, and we only serve beer and pizza, so it doesn't get too crazy.

But that particular night, I stepped out of the bar and almost stepped on something alive, and it barely dodged my foot. I know I would've squashed it. I shined my little keychain penlight on it and couldn't believe it, it was a badger!

I ran back in and got Josie, my sister, but by the time she came out I could see it trying to hide over under a small bush in the alley. We walked over and took a better look—yup, a badger, a very young one.

My mom once wrote a cute little story for her fourth graders called "Badger the Goodger," but I know badgers aren't very good. They can be mean little things, so we steered clear of it, wondering what a badger was doing in the middle of town. Neither of us had ever even seen one.

While wondering why a badger had come into town, we noticed flashing lights a few blocks away—a lot of flashing lights. Something was going on down by the river.

I decided to drive by there on my way home, just out of curiosity, and what I saw was a real bummer.

The river was rising and a bunch of people were sandbagging the houses along the riverfront. Police cars and fire trucks were lighting everything up for them, and everyone looked tired and frazzled. I sometimes forget that one a.m. isn't a normal time to be awake for most people.

I decided to stop and see if I could help. I offered to bring our big coffee machines over, if they could find a place to plug them in, and I called Josie. We were soon in business, running out of someone's garage.

We supplied free coffee and pizza for everyone sand-bagging, and Josie and I were busy until the next day, when we had to go home and get some sleep. Last I looked, the river was still rising and was almost to the sandbags.

That explained the little badger—its home was washed out and it was seeking higher ground. I felt bad for it and hoped it had found a new home.

The next afternoon, on my way down to the pizza bar, I swung by the river to see how things fared, but I couldn't even get down there.

The road was closed, and I could see the flood waters coming right up into the next street. It appeared all the sandbagged houses had been evacuated and probably flooded, in spite of everyone's efforts.

It had been raining for days, and though this was something the town had experienced before, it had been a number of years ago.

The town had been built along the Big Muddy River, where it served as headquarters for the timber mill that worked the big logs the loggers would send floating down from the thick forests in the mountains above.

The mill had long since closed, and the little town now was home to a small college, or it would have long ago died off.

There wasn't much anyone could do at this point except evacuate their homes, if they lived near the river. The rain was forecast to get more intense.

It was a one-hundred year flood, they were saying, but I noticed it hadn't been that long since the last big flood, maybe only 10 years. It seemed like these big floods were getting more common, and we'd had a small one just last year.

There were police and fire vehicles all over the place, and I was now worrying if the river might actually come up to where we were, as it was now only a couple of blocks down from us.

I stopped and asked a guy who looked like a firefighter what he thought, and he said if the rains continued, it just might flood us out. It wouldn't hurt to be prepared.

So I went to the bar and told Josie what I'd seen and heard. We decided to go ahead and open up and just kind of wait and see what happened.

We stood to lose a lot if the place flooded, as there was no way we could move our big pizza ovens or expensive espresso machine, not to mention tables and chairs and all that.

And of course we didn't have flood insurance, nobody did, it was too expensive. One just took their chances. We barely made enough to live on as it was.

We had plenty of business that afternoon. It seemed like everyone was all excited about the flood.

Part of the campus was down by the river and it had been cordoned off, though it was mostly ball fields and such. The rest of the campus was open for business, though the kids speculated what parts would close first if the river kept rising. They seemed to be kind of enjoying the excitement and were placing bets on what buildings would flood.

The drama department looked like it could be one of the first to go, and a few drama students were having pizza and beer while planning how to evacuate the costumes and equipment.

We were on lower ground than most of the college, so I was paying attention to the reports the kids brought in, believe me.

But one report was a bit out there. One of the kids, a student named Sarah, came bursting in saying a bear was stranded out on a bunch of flotsam in the middle of the river. She was all excited and wanted to do something to save it. It was wet and bedraggled looking and needed help.

This spurred a big discussion on how it would be impossible to rescue a bear from a raging river except by helicopter, followed by various theories on how to do that.

You could tranquilize it and then tie it to a gurney and lift it into the chopper, but what if it woke up early and all that. It was a pretty interesting and creative discussion, but Sarah finally gave up and left, possibly looking for real help.

I decided to go check it out, see if I could spot the poor bear and also see where the waters were. I was pretty worried about our bar—and I guess the bear, too.

I drove on down to the city park, which was along the river, or I should say was now under the river. I parked and got out, along with a dozen or so other people, standing on a small hill above where the park used to be.

Sarah was there, so I asked her about the bear. She pointed to a jumble of trees and logs that had snagged on a big rock in the river, and sure enough, there was something black out there, hanging on for dear life.

Some of the others were watching it, too, and voiced their concerns.

"Somebody should help that poor bear out there."

"How the hell could you help it? It would be a death wish to get on that river."

"Maybe somebody could throw it a rope."

"You'd need a 50 foot rope or more, and how would you get it out there? How would a bear hang onto a rope?"

And on and on. Sarah and I stood there together, feeling bad for the bear. I told her I wished I could do something for it. She agreed.

She added, "It's kind of odd looking. I was checking it out through my binoculars. I'm not actually convinced it's a bear."

I was shocked. "What else could it be?" I asked.

"I think it's a young Bigfoot." She kind of whispered this to me, not wanting anyone else to hear, handing me the binoculars.

It was hard to make out, but it was clinging to a big log that was snagged by another big log against a bunch of tree branches, all caught on a big rock in the middle of the river. The whole thing looked like it could go any minute.

I tried to see what the young animal looked like, but had no luck. But then it turned its head a bit, and I could see its face. It looked like a young person out there, but someone with hair on its face and a flattened nose. But it was not a bear. It looked tired and frightened. I couldn't believe what I was seeing.

"Sarah, if you're right. We're looking at an endangered animal struggling to survive, especially if it's a young one."

"I know," she answered glumly. "We have to help it. We just have to."

"Look at how big the river is. It's huge, there's no way you could get a boat out there, and that's the only way I would know to help it. Plus, it's a wild animal. It wouldn't know what was going on and would probably flee, drowning."

Sarah's answer surprised me. I guess she knew a lot more about Bigfoot than I did.

"Bigfoot's smart. It would know you were helping it. It wouldn't panic. It wouldn't hurt anybody. We've got to get out there and help it somehow."

"I'm game, Sarah, if you can figure out a way. Come on over to the pizza bar if you do. Right now it looks like it's pretty much stuck where it's at for awhile, but if the river gets much higher, it's going to wash everything off that rock it's snagged on. Maybe the animal can swim to shore."

"I don't know," Sarah replied, looking like she was about to cry. "What if one set out upstream in a boat and steered it down to the snag where the Bigfoot could jump in. Would it do it?"

"You'd have to be nuts to get on that river right now. Don't even think about it, Sarah. One big log and you'd be history. And I doubt if the animal would jump in, anyway, and it would only have a minute to do so, then you'd be swept past it. Or maybe snagged there too."

Sarah sighed, "You're right. I guess I need to remember that serenity prayer that says to change what you can and accept what you can't. I need to quit being such a bleeding heart. See you later."

I sensed a determination in Sarah, and I suspected she might be thinking about trying something really foolish to save that animal. Not much I could do about it, but I hoped I was wrong.

One last look at it and nothing had changed, it was still hanging on for dear life. It was dusk, and the river would rise during the night if all this rain kept up. I doubted if it would be there when dawn came.

But I had the pizza bar to focus on, so I drove back up there and got back to work.

About midnight, a firefighter came in and told us we had to evacuate, the river was coming up fast. We had thought about what we would do if this happened, but we still weren't prepared.

We started hauling off the stuff we could, the smaller things like the cash register and dishes. The students who were there really pitched in and helped, and I promised them all free pizza if the bar survived.

A couple of them drove pickups, and when we had everything that we could get out, we took everything over to the house and unloaded it all. It was a sinking feeling to stand there in the rain in the middle of the night looking at all we owned possibly being ruined, even though we had put tarps over it and brought the smaller things inside.

I somehow figured we were soon in for a career change. Sure enough, the bar flooded that night. Our beautiful pizza ovens were covered in black river mud the next time I saw them, and the big espresso machine was gone entirely, maybe floating on down to the ocean.

I couldn't help but wonder how the little Bigfoot was faring. Its plight somehow made me more appreciative of my own situation, dire as it was.

All we stood to lose was our livelihood, but the little animal stood to lose its life. It seemed sadder than seeing all our stuff lying wet on the ground.

I slept a little that night, but the excitement was too much, and I was up at dawn. I was worried about the little animal, whatever it was, and I wanted to go see if it had made it through the night. The way the river had risen, I was doubtful.

I drove on down to the park. The flooding was even more extensive now, and the river seemed to be rising even more.

It hadn't abated any at all. It was still raining. In fact, it was raining so hard I couldn't really see if the flotsam snag with the little animal on it was even still out there.

I went to check on the bar. I should've been more worried about it than the animal, as I somehow knew it was history, and sure enough, it was. I couldn't even get near the building.

The flooding had covered blocks of the downtown, and the bar was a good three blocks in. The police had everything cordoned off. I knew the water had to be deep and the damage extensive.

I was glad we didn't own the building, but rented. Our only loss was the equipment, at least. Others had lost much much more.

I felt kind of shellshocked. I went back home, telling Josie about everything. The town was continuing to flood. The city had now asked people to open their doors to others, as the shelters were full. And it was still raining.

I tried to nap, but I knew they needed help downtown sandbagging and evacuating. But my heart wasn't in it any more. I just wanted to get away from everything. I think, in retrospect, that I was in a bit of shock.

I told my sister I was going for a drive out in the country to get away and wouldn't be gone long. She understood. She had been cleaning what we'd salvaged from the bar and was in shock herself.

I drove out past the park on into the forest, down towards the big clearcut area where the mill had stored logs, and then onto a little road that led out to where someone was building a vacation home. I had to stop when the pavement ended, as the road was nothing but mud from all the rain.

I just set there, by the side of the road, thinking about what had happened. I was still worried about that little Bigfoot, wondering if it had survived, when a plan came to me.

Old mill towns have lots of history, and our town was no exception. Some of that history included a big cable that had once been used to cross the river before a bridge was built.

A small boat was attached to the cable and pulled across. That cable was still there, although the boat was long gone.

Why couldn't we rig this up and get a boat out to the little animal? Whether or not it was smart enough to get into the boat was another question, but at least we would have tried.

I guess deep inside I was a bleeding heart just like Sarah. I turned around and went back to town.

How could I find Sarah? I had no idea where she lived. I would just have to make the plan work without her help and inspiration. But first, I needed to see if the little animal was even still there. I drove back down to the park.

I guess great minds think alike, cause Sarah was there, along with a dozen other students, and a small boat bobbed out by the flotsam snag, attached to the old cable.

She had been miles ahead of me, and she'd managed to pull it off. Everyone was standing there in suspense. Would the animal get into the boat?

Sarah saw me and smiled, and I decided it was a waste of time to tell her I'd had the same idea, so I just gave her a high five.

She handed me her binoculars, and I had the pleasure of watching the animal climb into the boat. I reported what I saw, and everyone cheered.

I love college kids, they are so enthusiastic and nothing stops them from doing what they want. They're too young and inexperienced to know they can't do something, they just go ahead and do it anyway.

The boat had ropes attached to pull it along the cable, and the plan had been that, if the young Bigfoot did get into the boat, they would pull it across to the side opposite town so it had a chance to go back into the forest.

Would it stay in the boat while they pulled it across? Would the current be too strong for them?

The boat started slowly moving across the river, slapping against the waves as it went, the little animal staying put inside. Everyone held their breath as Sarah, who now had the binoculars, reported on the progress.

The boat was now safely on the other side! There were a bunch of college guys over there, pulling the boat in, and they stood back, allowing the animal to jump out and flee.

They later reported it was the mangiest bear they'd ever seen and had a weird face. I don't think they had a clue what they'd helped rescue. The little Bigfoot ran like a banshee for the forest and quickly disappeared while everyone on my side of the river cheered.

I congratulated Sarah. She was now calling it a bear, and I think she decided to not say what it really was. She just wanted to see it rescued and then be left alone. I admired that, as we both knew it was best for the animal.

The rains finally stopped, and the town eventually recovered, taking weeks to clean everything up. Our espresso machine was found in the neighbor's building and actually still worked after we cleaned it up.

Our landlord cleaned up the building, we cleaned up our ovens, and two months later, we reopened the pizza bar.

We had a new menu item—Sarah's Bigfoot Boat Float—which, as I'm sure you've noticed, is the biggest and best root beer float you can get anywhere.

[9] The Night Hikers

The fellow who told this story was a fairly intense individual, and I thought I might have a hard time guiding him on a flyfishing trip, as I'm usually a pretty mellow guy. I wasn't sure if he could relax enough to have a good time and enjoy the fishing.

It was his first time out, and he ended up really liking it. When he told us this tale around the campfire, I got a little glimpse into his character. He was intense, but not ashamed to admit to being afraid, like some guys are, and he turned out to be a really humble fellow who had practically driven himself to the brink of a nervous breakdown, he later told me. That was before he discovered flyfishing, of course. At his request, only very general information is included in this story.

My name is Carl, and I used to like to climb things. I've climbed a lot of big peaks and I usually would go solo, as I like my own pace and solitude.

My story is pretty simple, but it scared me a lot.

I was camped at around 11,000 feet (according to my topo) in a high mountain meadow in the Wind River Range of Wyoming.

I was going to get up early the next day and climb two peaks, both somewhat close together. Both were tough climbs.

I had arrived late in the evening and set up my little tent next to the trail in a little clearing. This was about 10 years ago almost to the day, July 4th.

I was started up a high pass, on the hill above the big meadow at the base of the pass, which I could see down below me. I didn't want to camp there, as it felt too open.

When you go solo all the time, you naturally become a bit wary and try to keep a low profile. It becomes second nature.

When you come up the trail, at one point you have to cross a pretty wild stream. I don't know if there's a bridge now, but at that time the old wooden bridge had collapsed and you had to cross on fallen logs and rocks, and it's a bit hairy, especially with a big pack on, as it's almost a waterfall at that point.

It's usually still pretty roily this time of year with runoff. I made the crossing with no problems, but went slow.

So, I got there at dusk and set up my tent and went to bed. I remember seeing the alpenglow on the peaks above me and thinking it was a shame I was so tired. I'd wanted to stay up and look at the night sky, but I was exhausted. No idea why, as I was in good shape and it's only a few miles up there, but not that bad, maybe six or seven.

I also remember thinking how quiet it was and contrasting that to what I knew was going on all over the country, the fireworks and noise. I quickly fell asleep.

I woke up suddenly in the middle of the night in a complete dread. It was so bad I immediately got up and started dressing. I knew I had to get out of there now, something bad was going to happen.

I was ready to take my tent down and stuff everything into my backpack, and then I slowed down enough to remember the stream crossing. There was no way I could do that at night.

I was in a quandary. I knew I had to get out of there, yet I had no idea why. I forced myself to crawl back into the tent and lay there, and it was a monumental task, given my mental state.

I was terrified but had no idea why. I was beginning to panic. I've never panicked before or since, so it was a very scary feeling.

As I lay there, unable to sleep and forcing myself to not get up and flee, I heard something coming down the trail.

The dread intensified. Whatever it was, it was walking on two feet, and it was big. My first thought was a bear. I just lay there very still.

Whatever this was came closer and closer to my tent, then stopped. I could now hear at least one more coming, maybe two, crunching on the small rocks on the trail, then silence.

You have no idea how terrifying something like that can be until you've experienced it. I don't go armed, too much extra weight to carry, plus I don't care much for guns. So I was pretty much defenseless.

I just lay there, and whatever it was just stood there.

I decided I had to see what was going on or I was going to have a full-on panic attack, so I very slowly and quietly sat up, then angled around to where I could peek out the tent door hopefully without being seen.

There was no moonlight of any kind, but I could make out three very large creatures standing above my tent, looking down at me in silence against a backdrop of incredible night sky, thick with stars.

The night visitors looked huge, and I estimated they were at least seven or eight feet tall, and they were all black. They were not bears.

They then just as quietly moved off, going on down the trail. As they passed, they seemed even bigger. They walked as if they could see quite well in the dark.

I don't really recall much after that, except waking up to a beautiful blue sky, and when I finally was awake and could remember what happened, feeling a sense of having had a weird dream.

But I knew I'd been awake. My stuff sack for my sleeping bag had been pulled from my backpack, and I remembered doing that, getting ready to pack up and leave during the night. I knew it wasn't a dream and puzzled over it.

I finally got up and packed everything up and went ahead on up the pass.

I then decided to forego climbing, as I was too tired, so I crested the pass and stood there looking down on the huge valley that separates the two big peaks I had wanted to climb.

I was suddenly deflated and just sat down in the tundra.

The previous night's events had taken their toll. All I wanted to do was go home. I felt tired.

I turned around and headed back down the pass.

I have no idea who or what the three creatures were, but I do know that I saw something. I've since read that Bigfoot can supposedly produce infrasound, which has the exact effects I had that night.

It's also possible it was altitude sickness, who knows?

But to this day I prefer not to hike in the Wind River Range. Why? The creatures did me no harm.

It's hard to explain, but now I know my world is shared with these other creatures, and I don't want to meet them again.

[10] The Hounds of Mist

· ·

I'll never forget Hank telling this story over a nice mellow fire one evening in the Colorado Rockies. He was a retired animal control officer (dogcatcher) from up in Oregon, though he didn't look old enough to be retired.

I had a hard time believing his story, especially the ending. It seemed too good to be true, but Hank assured me it all really happened. He said that when dogs pack together like that, they're easier to catch, as they all just mindlessly follow the pack leader.

Of course, their real pack leader was nowhere around at their crucial moment of capture, but was out howling somewhere in the woods. But I guess I'd better just let you read the story before I end up giving it all away.

For many years I worked as the animal control officer for a small town deep in the Oregon forests called Mist. It's a pretty little town, when you can see it. It's aptly named.

I took pride in my job. I wasn't the dreaded dogcatcher type, I actually was the only person working animal control, so I had a lot of latitude in how I handled things. I was even voted Animal Control Officer of the Year for the state, because people liked me and knew I loved animals.

I tried to handle situations with care and compassion. I bet I was one of the few officers who actually relocated skunks, for example.

Anyway, my name is Hank, and I'm now retired, but I'd like to tell you a story about the strangest thing I've ever seen in my entire life, and I was right in the thick of it. It happened in the summer of 1997.

The whole thing started with a call from Mrs. Johnson. She lived over on Seventh Street, which was right smack in the middle of town.

I mention this because it threw us off as to what was really going on. If it had been on the edge of town, we might have had more of a clue.

She called about 10 p.m. to tell me her little Pekinese dog was missing. She'd let him out about an hour earlier and now the little guy was just plain gone.

She had a fenced yard, so there was no way he could've gotten out. She'd spent the past hour calling and searching for him, and would I come over and help her out?

I was about ready to go to bed, but such is the nature of my job. Sometimes I miss talking to everyone around town, but usually I'm glad I'm retired when I think of nights like this. It also happened to be raining. Like I said, Mist was aptly named.

I went straight over there. She was in tears, just beside herself. I drove around the neighborhood with my spotlight for an hour with no luck.

I also would get out and walk some, calling, "Here Precious," with no luck.

I felt really bad for the old gal. That dog was her only family. Later, after everything was settled, she actually left her house to the local Humane Society, which was a really great thing to do.

She also left me a small amount, about a thousand dollars, but I didn't feel right taking it, so I donated it to them also.

When I went back to her house, she'd been crying, and I just felt awful for her. All I could think was that maybe a coyote had jumped the fence and taken the little dog, but I sure didn't want to tell her that.

I tried to console her, saying we would start the search again in the morning, but for her to leave the gate open in case he came back.

It was probably giving her false hope, but it was all I could do.

The next day, I went back over there, and she'd been up all night looking for and calling the little dog, but he had just plain disappeared.

I drove around some more, mostly to make her feel better, and she went to everyone's house in the neighborhood telling them to keep an eye out, even offered a big $100 reward. After that, she put posters all over town with his photo and the reward offer.

I would see her out every once in awhile, looking for him, afterward. This was one of the harder parts of my job, when animals got lost or came up missing.

The next incident of that nature came three nights later, when another dog came up missing, also in mid-town.

This time it was a bit earlier when I got the call, about 7 p.m. This was a bit more puzzling, as the dog, Shep, was too big to be coyote bait, and since the owner didn't have a fenced yard, he would put Shep on a tie-out when he needed to go out.

He said Shep hadn't been out more than 10 minutes when he went to let him back in, and he was gone. This dog was a big shepherd mix and was kind of territorial, so it wasn't likely anyone would take him, as he would've scared most people off.

The owner was really upset. Shep was getting old and couldn't do well on his own, he had a bit of arthritis.

I was really puzzled by this one. All I could figure was that the owner had thought he'd closed the snap and hadn't, and the dog had gotten away and was running around like dogs do when they get their freedom.

So I drove around town, looking for him, but no luck.

Two dogs missing in a town of about 100 dogs within the space of three days. Not really enough to be suspicious, but still...

Now I was seeing another missing dog poster around town, this one for Shep, and I'd still run into poor Mrs. Johnson out looking for Precious. It broke my heart, and I sure wished I could find both dogs.

Several nights later, another call, but not for a missing dog, thankfully. This call was a bit on the weird side, but I went out anyway.

It was out on the edge of town at the home of a local businessman, Joe, who owned a local restaurant. He had a good reputation, didn't drink, and I had to take his call seriously, even though I didn't want to.

"Officer," he said as we stood out in his yard in the dark, "I could swear there's something out there calling. It's actually more like a howl, and it sure isn't coyotes. There seem to be a couple of them, and it's like they're calling to each other."

He continued, "One seems to be over by the old dump and the other out in that grove of cedar trees. It really spooked me, for sure, and it went on for about two hours. The sound really carried, like it's big. I was hoping if you came out you could hear it and give me your opinion."

We stood there for quite awhile and heard nothing. But that night, two dogs went missing, both beagles, Jake and Callie, and from the same house where they'd been in a kennel in a garage.

The garage was locked. The lock had been twisted off, not cut with boltcutters like a burglar would do, but just twisted completely off. The owner hadn't heard a sound from the dogs, who typically would have barked their beagle noses off, he said.

Two days later, it was Sammy and Spot, two large mutts who both lived on the south side of town, but with different owners and in different houses.

Six missing dogs out of approximately 100. That was six percent, which was becoming more statistically significant.

Now I was beginning to think the dogs were being stolen, but who would steal a random bunch of dogs, even breaking in to do so? Why steal a dog, when they were practically free for the taking at the Humane Society?

I thought of someone taking the dogs to sell to a research lab, but the nearest lab was in California.

None of this made any sense, but I decided it was time to warn the local townspeople of what was happening so they could exercise caution. I called the newspaper.

They sent Kath down, which I knew they would, since she was the only reporter.

I told her we needed to get the word out that maybe someone was stealing dogs so people could be careful at night with their pets.

She jumped right on it, which I knew she would, but I didn't suspect the tact she would take in mangling the story until I got a call from Joe the next day, the guy who had heard the howling from his back yard.

"Hank, hows come you to decide there's some strange beast out there and not even get back to me on it, since I'm the one who called it in?" He sounded a bit miffed.

I had no idea what he was talking about until he read me Kath's front-page story about the missing dogs and how a wild beast was suspected.

I moaned out load, though I didn't mean to.

"Oh for cryin' out loud," I responded. "I told her about the howling so she would tell people to be careful, but I sure as heck didn't say it was a wild beast stealing dogs."

Now I was the one who was miffed, especially when I had to field concerned calls from Mrs. Johnson and half the town. The truth of the matter was, Kath was probably right, but no one knew it.

The next night, I got a call from Dispatch around midnight. I usually get calls direct from townspeople concerned about some skunk or whatever, and when Dispatch calls, I know it's something serious.

They asked me to get right out to Joe's house, where there had been some strange goings-on. I was soon there, where I was told there'd been a break-in, but nothing was stolen. I wondered why the animal control officer had been called for a break-in.

Joe was standing there talking to the police officer, Terry, who was trying to fingerprint a doorknob that was nothing more than a twisted piece of metal lying on the ground.

"Whatever it was, it was big and strong," Joe reported, fear in his eyes. "Hank, I know it had to be that beast thing we heard howling, I just know it."

"What did it do, come inside?" I asked.

"Come in and I'll show you," Joe answered. I stepped inside.

"This is why I called you," Terry added, then went to her police car to write up her report, lights flashing.

Joe's wife stood there, holding something wrapped in a towel, something small and apparently alive.

"The thing broke the door open, shoved this poor little guy in, then closed the door and left, at least that's all we can figure out," Joe's wife, Millie, said. "I have no idea what to do with the poor little thing, it's a mess."

She handed me the bundle, which I took, unwrapping the towel. It was Precious. He was a bit on the scrawny side and covered head to toe in weeds and small sticks, all matted into his fine coat, but otherwise he looked fine.

He wagged his tail like someone who'd been caught sneaking sips of cooking wine while the cook was out, like he was guilty of something or other.

I couldn't believe my eyes. I asked for a repeat of the story, but it was still unbelievably simple: something had broken in and left Precious, but taken nothing and damaged nothing other than the doorknob. Joe and his wife were upset, but no harm done.

I took the little dog, thanked them, and went straight to Mrs. Johnson's house, where I had to bang on the door for ten minutes to wake her up. She nearly had a heart attack when she saw Precious, as did Precious. The happiness on both sides was tangible.

I explained what I could, told Mrs. Johnson to get the dog to a groomer first thing in the morning, then went home and back to bed, but not back to sleep.

First thing in the morning, I got a call from Joe, which I had half expected. He wanted to know how the little dog was, so I told him he had been returned to a very happy owner.

As we were talking, I could hear Millie yelling something at him in the background. Joe was quiet for a moment, then said, "I think you'd better get back out here, Hank," then hung up.

I hadn't even had my morning coffee yet. I poured the rest of yesterday's pot into a cup and stuck it in the microwave just as the phone rang again. It was Kath. She'd heard last night's call on her police receiver and wanted to know what had happened.

I told her to meet me at Joe's, as I took the cup of stale coffee from the microwave. Might as well let her in on whatever was happening out there, that way I wouldn't have to tell her later.

Besides, maybe she was onto something about the beast stealing the dogs. I was tired and about ready to hand her the case. I just wanted to go back to relocating skunks.

We both arrived at Joe's at the same time. He and Millie were waiting on the porch. Nobody said a word, not even good morning. I think we were all just about fried.

We silently followed Millie around to the side of the house, where she pointed at the ground.

"You've had a Bigfoot visitor," Kath said. "You and the Millers down the road. I photographed the same thing over at their place a few days ago. The tracks look identical."

"Bigfoot? At Miller's? Why didn't you tell me, Kath?" I asked, a bit miffed again.

"Because I know you don't believe in them, and I'm working on a story about how they're stealing dogs. And I know you think it's craziness, but that's exactly what's going on."

Now she sounded miffed. Joe and Millie looked incredulous and a bit scared.

"So, you think a Bigfoot broke into the house and left the dog?" Joe asked Kath. I seemed to quickly be losing my authority here, I was no longer the one in the know.

"What dog?" she asked. Joe then explained the previous night's events, while she took notes. She acted more like she was the investigating officer, but I didn't care. I was ready to give her my job if she wanted it.

"Kath," I interjected, "Why would a Bigfoot steal a dog and then return it to the wrong house?"

"Easy," she answered. "It's been spying on the town's dogs and it wanted this one, thought it was cute, maybe. But it found out that a little dog with a fine coat was too hard to care for, and it sure couldn't run with the big dogs, so it returned it to the nearest house. I doubt if Bigfoot has much of a sense of pet ownership. Or any kind of ownership, for that matter."

It made sense, if one believed in Bigfoot, which I probably didn't. I was more inclined to think some human had stolen the dog and then got rid of it by breaking into Joe and Millie's. A Bigfoot would have probably just eaten the little dog, I figured.

Why the twisted doorknob? I didn't know, but maybe they were just a strong and impatient person who didn't know how to pick a lock.

That made more sense to me than conjuring up a mythological monster to explain it away. And the tracks? Obviously a hoax. And the howling? Also a hoax, probably a bunch of kids having fun and totally unrelated to the break-in.

"OK, Kath," I wasn't going to give up that easily. "Why would a Bigfoot steal dogs in the first place?"

"That I don't know," she answered quietly. "But we need to find those dogs, Hank." She gave me a look of impatience, like I needed to do a better job, then thanked Joe and Millie and drove off.

I also thanked them, reminded them that Bigfoot was just a legend and probably didn't even exist, said I'd be in touch, and drove away, heading back home for a decent cup of coffee and some breakfast.

As much as I hated to admit it, Kath's theory made sense as events progressed. More stolen dogs, but never another small one, they were all large.

By now, the entire town was abuzz with Bigfoot talk, and everyone was guarding their dogs like their dogs were supposed to be guarding them. It seemed like the roles had been reversed.

Before long, I expected the dogs to be running the town, with the people doing whatever the dogs wanted them to do. But wait, it had been like that for a long time already. Why else would one have to pay for an ice-cream cone at the Velvet Cream Drive-In while the doggies got a free sample?

The stolen dog calls dropped off completely, but now the calls to come out and investigate weird sounds and howling increased.

One night, I got a call from Buzz, the owner of Shep. He was still mourning his old dog and had been glum every time I saw him, but now he was all excited.

"Hank, I'm out here at the plane park, and I can hear a bunch of dogs barking out on the edge of the forest, and they sound like they're packed up, and I swear to God I can hear Shep's voice. He has a very distinct bark, I've never heard anything like it."

I was soon out at the model airplane field, where people went to fly their hobby craft. Buzz sat there in the dark on the tailgate of his little Nissan pickup, where I joined him.

"They just veered off into the woods as you drove up," he said. "Let's just sit here for a bit and see if they come back. I know that was Shep." Buzz looked like he was wiping his eyes with his sleeve, but it was hard to tell in the dark.

We sat there for a good half-hour when I'll be damned if we couldn't hear what sounded like a pack of dogs in the distance, with a strange resonant howling sometimes vibrating above the pack noise.

"God almighty," I whispered. "What if Kath's right?"

Buzz knew exactly what I was talking about.

"She is right," he answered quietly. "Listen, hear that sort of high crazy-sounding bark? That's Shep, I know it. The old guy's going to have a heart attack, he's too old to be running wild like that." Buzz's sleeve went back up to his eyes.

I refused to believe any of it, but I didn't say anything to Buzz. The whole thing was outlandish and had no logic to it of any kind. Why would a Bigfoot steal town dogs and then run them in a pack? Why didn't the dogs escape and run home?

These were dogs used to the lap of luxury, why would they run around half-wild? Who was feeding them? And the bit I'd read about Bigfoot indicated that they usually killed dogs, not stole them and had wild escapades running around with them in the dark. It was pure insanity.

The barking was getting louder. The hounds were heading our way!

"I dunno about you, Buzz, but I think it's best we get into our vehicles. Wild dogs have been known to do some wild things."

Buzz nodded, and we both got into my truck. We had the windows rolled down, and we could hear the pack definitely getting closer. It was an eerie feeling, knowing a pack of possibly wild animals was coming our way, even though I was armed and we were both in a vehicle. Buzz didn't look a bit worried, just excited.

Soon, the pack sounded like it was very close, and sure enough, one bark stood out from the rest. I swore I could also hear a couple of beagles, as they have a very distinct baying noise. Could Kath be right? Were these the missing dogs?

All of a sudden, Buzz jumped out of the truck and started yelling as loud as he could, calling Shep and whistling.

I was pretty scared at that point, cause the pack was now right at the edge of the little landing strip, not more than one-hundred feet from us, and Buzz was outside yelling for Shep.

I yelled at Buzz to get in, but he didn't, and instead he started out towards the strip. I had a bad feeling about it, as the dogs were now coming in, barking and baying like lost souls.

"Shep! Shep! C'mere, Shep!"

Now Buzz was surrounded by dogs, as quick as one could say siccum. I had to do something, so I jumped out and ran over to where the pack now circled him, my bear spray handy.

Buzz was down on the ground, and dogs were jumping all over him. I had no idea what to do. I couldn't spray cause I might hit Buzz. I could hear him groaning, and now the dogs were coming for me!

Before I could hit the bear spray button, I was down, dogs jumping all over me and wagging their tails, licking me like I was their long-lost owner.

Now Buzz was up, calling the dogs off me and whistling, and he opened the back of my truck and they all jumped in. He quickly shut the door, locking the entire bunch into the back of my animal control truck.

I later counted eight, every missing dog in town was there, except Precious, of course, as he was no longer missing. And Buzz had quickly slipped a leash on old Shep.

Buzz was now hooting and hollering, and Shep was dancing around him, the pair jumping up and down. Shep's arthritis was apparently cured.

I had no idea what to do or think. I felt like I'd just been an unwitting character in a bizarre movie. It was just too unreal. Finally, Shep was safely in Buzz's truck, and Buzz came over to where I was standing, still stunned.

"Kath was right," he said quietly.

"Good thinking on the dogs," I replied. "True genius."

We both just stood there, not knowing what to say.

Just then, a low weird howling came from the edge of the cedar trees, a sound I will never forget. The back of my truck exploded with dogs madly barking and trying to get out.

"We need to get the hell out of here now!" Buzz said, and we were both quickly in our vehicles and driving fast, back to town.

The dogs were going crazy in the back of my truck, yipping and howling and making so much noise that I was worried they would get in a big dog fight. I beelined straight for the sheriff's office while calling Dispatch. I needed help, even though Buzz was following me.

It was the most dogs I'd ever brought in, and I think I may have set a record. We eventually got everyone sorted out and into kennels, where we could assess things and figure out who was who.

The dogs looked pretty good, considering. They had sore pads and were mangy looking and thin, but they seemed to be in good spirits. They reminded me of my nephews after they get back from a two-week backpacking adventure. Tired, but happy.

The dogs were eventually all returned to their happy owners, who now guarded them like never before, taking them to the drive-in for free ice cream and that sort of thing. But it wasn't over yet.

Kath, of course, covered the story, plastering it all over the front page, and Buzz and I were heroes. But the townspeople were now convinced there was at least one Bigfoot hanging around, maybe more, and there was talk about what to do to prevent a repeat.

Joe and Millie were still scared stiff and were thinking of leaving their house, so Kath figured their place would be a good base to start the Bigfoot Go Home Campaign. She had conjured the whole plan up and was now the Field Commander.

Buzz was also involved, saying he never wanted to lose Shep again. In fact everyone who had lost a dog was involved, even Mrs. Johnson, who manned the walkie-talkies.

Kath had managed to get several boxes of M80s from the Department of Wildlife, and the Bigfoot Battalion spent several nights lobbing them into the forest from various parts of the edge of town. It was a noisy enterprise, and a number of people complained, but the Battalion soon ran out of ammo and the war was over.

I guess it was successful, as no one ever mentioned seeing a Bigfoot again, to my knowledge, and no dogs went suspiciously missing.

I never did understand why a Bigfoot would steal dogs in the first place, but Kath maintained that it wanted to let them run free, just like Bigfoot itself did, that it felt sorry for them.

Run free? Maybe. We all long to run free at various points in our lives. Who knows?

I personally think the Bigfoot was training the dogs to flush out deer and rabbits and such for its dinner.

Did this mean I now believed in Bigfoot?

Not necessarily, but I will say that I try to keep an open mind, as I know there was something out there, stealing dogs and howling in the wind.

Whatever it was, it sure couldn't deal with a dog named Precious.

[11] At the Office

The next story came to me one evening from a totally unexpected source—my camp cook. I had hired Lance to help with the dutch-oven cooking my trips are so well-known for, and he was a real pro. I had no idea he used to do office work, as he seemed so at ease outdoors and really knew his stuff.

His story is a bit sad at first, but it shows how a change of attitude can really turn one's life around. He was happy to share his philosophy with us around the campfire, and here's the story he told.

This was a few years back when my wife and I split up, and I ended up living in my office. I can tell you that was a very depressing time for me, for sure. She kicked me out of the house, as I had taken up drinking again after a five-year hiatus, and she was fed up.

I don't blame her, but I just had too much stress going on and that was my escape. I'm totally off the stuff now, and I can say I wasn't drinking when any of this happened.

So, she was living in our nice big house, and I had my office. I couldn't afford any place else cause I was still making the house payment.

It's a little stand-alone building right on Main Street, kind of sinking into the ground on one side and at least 100 years old. It has a big lot behind it that's nothing but weeds, but does give a little privacy.

I didn't want anyone to know I was living there, as it's not zoned residential, and I was afraid I'd get a code violation, so I was kind of laying low the entire time, parking around back. The building next door was abandoned.

My office had one big room and a bathroom, and that was it—and big windows, which made it hard to sneak around until I covered them with tarps. I set a cot up in one corner and put a sleeping bag and a pad on it, and that was my new place.

No lights at night, cause I didn't want to get busted by code enforecement, so I would just sit there in the dark and watch the cars and trucks go by, wondering how I got there and where everyone else was going, wishing I was them or at the very least, with them. I had a little light come in from the neons of the little burger joint across the street, but when they shut down at ten p.m. every night, so did I. Bedtime.

Then I would lie there and listen to the big trucks going by, maybe 30 feet from my head, as the building was right on the edge of Main Street. I hoped nobody ever decided to crash through the wall.

Nobody ever came to visit because nobody knew I was there. Even though it was my office, I didn't run the kind of business that people would come to. My job was coordinating trucking shipments by phone and fax, and I never saw nobody.

Now this was a little town, and right across the street next to the burger joint was a somewhat seedy motel, though it had seen better days. It was called the Robber's Hideaway, after some outlaws who had robbed a bank 50 miles away and probably never set foot in our little town.

I watched some people come and go from that place that would wish I hadn't, if they knew. But I'm not the type to get involved in other people's business, as I can't even manage my own.

Sometimes a car would go through the drive-through of the burger joint, and as they sat there, their car lights would shine directly into where I was sitting, which was a bit irritating. And sometimes I would sit and watch the kids running the joint, watch the customers come in, I was that bored.

When the burger joint shut down their lights for the night, I would hang up my tarps so nobody would see me sleeping if they happened to walk by, which nobody ever did, to my knowledge. It was a very quiet part of a dying little town.

The one thing that I did like, that brought me some comfort, was seeing people go by in their big RVs. I would think about what kind I'd like to have. As I was going to sleep, I would pretend I was going to buy one the next day, and that seemed to keep me from being too depressed. I wondered where everyone got their money.

So, every night I'd crawl into my sleeping bag on the cot and try to sleep. The office didn't have much for heat, so it would usually take awhile for me to get warm, then I would drift off.

The next morning I'd be so stiff and sore I could barely move. I'd get up, make some coffee, wash up a bit, and be right back at it, working, sometimes not even shaving until late morning. It was a helluva way to live.

After a week or so of this, I was getting pretty desperate. I was as lonely as any guy in a country-western song, and it seemed I never went anywhere. I was getting more and more depressed, and now my wife had filed for divorce, so it didn't look like things would be getting any better soon.

It seemed the nights were the worst, so I decided I needed to get out, be outside, get some new perspective. But where to go? I wasn't a bar type, in spite of drinking, which I'd stopped for good anyway.

I was missing my family, but they were all long gone, and I started wishing for the days when I was young, when being outdoors was a big part of my life, when my dad and I would drive all over the country, just exploring the old roads.

I decided I'd get out and start driving around and see what was out there, even if it was evening before I could start because of work and all.

I started out just driving around town, up and down the residential streets, but that just made me miss having a home. So I branched out and started driving the country roads, out where the farms are.

That wasn't much better, it just made me feel lonelier. I headed for the backroads, out in the woods where nobody was, but that just spooked me, wondering what was out there.

I hadn't accomplished a thing, I was still just as lonely as ever. What I needed was my own place, even a small apartment, where I could fix myself dinner and watch a little TV, even have a friend over occasionally.

This office was about as bleak as you can get, no wonder I was more and more depressed. But I had no extra money at all, it was all going to keep the house from going into foreclosure until the judge could decide who got what.

I decided to try walking around town. It would be good for me, help me get rid of my bit of a paunch and get me outside at the same time.

So, I tried to start a little routine. I would have dinner at the burger joint since I couldn't cook in my office, then I'd go kick back for an hour or so, then I'd walk around town. I'd make it into an exercise thing and walk so long every night.

That would be good for me. I would feel like maybe I was going somewhere. I'd walk until I was tired, then come home and go to bed. That way I'd avoid that lonely heart-break-hotel feeling that was causing me so much pain.

I started that very night. I walked down Main Street, over to the park, then along the street to the community church, then on around back to Main. Each night, I'd go a bit further.

The first night, I felt much better. There's something about walking that is more intimate than driving, you can take the time to really examine things, and the physical nature of it leaves your mind free to think.

I did a lot of thinking on those walks, believe me. The only bad thing about the walks was having to go back to the office. I was getting to where I hated that place.

One night about two weeks into this new enterprise, while I was walking along, I got the feeling I was being followed. Now, I'm a big guy, and I don't worry too much, as I can take care of myself. I'd been in a few bar fights in my youth, and I knew how to win.

But this idea of being followed kind of bothered me, so I quickly ducked down an alley and changed directions. I headed back to the office, but then it occurred to me that whoever was following me might go right along, and I didn't want anyone hanging around there, it was too isolated, down there all alone all night. I didn't want anyone to know I was there.

So, I decided to walk on over to Ruth's Cafe and hang out a bit until whoever it was gave up, then go on back to the office. I did that, and when I left, I still had this weird feeling I was being watched and followed.

I wasn't sure what to do, so I just went on back to the office, but instead of going inside, I left it locked up and got in my car and drove off. I ended up spending the night on my buddy Jim's couch.

The next night, I went ahead with the walk, as I wanted to see if I would feel that way again. I walked around a bit, senses heightened, then went into the burger joint, as it was still open. I had once again felt like I was being followed.

I hadn't seen anyone either time, and I was beginning to think I was just paranoid. But for some reason I didn't feel comfortable going to the office, I don't know why. And I stayed at Jim's again.

I couldn't just move in to Jim's. I had to figure out what was going on. I decided to just stay at the office the next night and see how it felt, not go for a walk or anything.

I was just sitting there, watching the trucks go by, when I saw something really big and dark quickly pass the front of the building and duck into the rear. I can tell you this really scared me after all that had been going on.

I quietly checked the locks, making sure the doors were secure, and I wished I had Jim's dog along with me. He was a border collie and a good watchdog.

I just set there in the dark, and then I started to hear what sounded like someone talking, though far away. In fact, it sounded like a party, people's voices visiting together and all, but far in the distance. Then I heard what sounded like monkey chatter, but also far away.

I was now really perplexed. What in the heck was going on? I had that same feeling of being watched, though there wasn't anyway anyone could see into the building, as I'd put the tarps up. I wished I had cut the tall weeds on that back lot, as it made a perfect place to hide.

I now quietly called Jim and told him what was going on, and he said he'd be right over. I was too scared to even go get in my car, and I couldn't call the police, since I wasn't supposed to be sleeping there.

I heard him drive up to the front door, and I was soon out the door and in his car, leaving the building locked up. Another night on his couch for me. He hadn't seen a thing.

The next day, I called a landscape place and had them come and cut down all the tall weeds on that back lot. It was a start at making the place less creepy, I thought.

I was fine there during the day, but as soon as night fell, I got weirded out. I was determined to not stay at Jim's that night, but to tough it out at the office. I didn't want to wear out my welcome.

I ended up in the Robber's Hideaway after hearing something scratching the walls outside. It wasn't like mice or any kind of animal, it was long scratching that started at the top of the wall and went clear to the bottom. Somebody had to be tall to do that.

I had no idea why anything would want to scare me. Could it be my soon-to-be-ex-wife putting someone up to it? It was totally unlike anything she would do. I actually called and talked to her about it.

She was very civil and said I needed to get out of there, but she didn't offer the spare room at the house. She then added that I should quit drinking. We were back to square one. She never believed anything I said, it seemed.

That afternoon, as I was sitting there working, I got mad, just plain mad. I had enough problems going on that I didn't need any more, and whoever was messing with my mind was going to be sorry.

I didn't deserve to have to live like this. I'd always done my best, and even when it was a bit short, I'd tried.

I missed my nightly walks, and I decided I wasn't going to let anyone take that from me. Those walks had been my only sanity through it all.

So, that evening, I went for a nice long walk. I was now carrying a small .22 pistol in my pocket, and that made me feel better, though I knew I would be seriously under-armed if something really big came after me. But so far, I hadn't seen anything but that fleeting moment of something running past the front window.

I now had started parking my car in the front, next to the door, under the streetlight, where I could make a getaway while seeing if anyone was there. But this time I had no intention of leaving. I was going to put on my warpaint and make a stand, I'd had enough.

My walk went well until I got over by the church, then I felt like something was watching me again. The community church has a big thicket behind it, where the creek comes through town, and it's always been kind of spooky and mysterious over there.

I didn't go any closer than about a half-block from it, as it was too dark and scary. The more I thought about it, that seemed to be where this feeling always started, when I got in the area of the thicket.

So, I just stopped and stood there for awhile, looking around. I then noticed someone in the shadows by the church, or rather, I should say I noticed someone smoking a cigarette, as I could see it glowing in the dark.

I stood there, watching, and the smoker did the same. But then it moved, and I could now see two cigarettes. That just seemed really weird to me, why would someone smoke two cigarettes? And it wasn't two people, they were too close together. It's funny how your mind holds onto a paradigm and won't let go, even when the truth is right there.

It finally dawned on me that what I was seeing were eyes glowing in the dark! Now I felt a chill go up my spine, and the hairs on the back of my neck literally stood up.

I don't think I've ever been so scared. The scratching on the walls was nothing compared to this. My heart rate went way up, and I could barely suck in a breath. For a few seconds, I didn't dare move.

Whatever this thing was, it was tall, because those eyes were a good two feet higher than mine, and like I said, I'm a big guy at 6'3".

I know it's bad to show fear in a situation like that, but I must have been emanating it, I was so scared. I realized I had my hand in my pocket, fingering my loaded gun, so I decided it might be prudent to show that gun. It might be a good deterrent.

I've been told to never reveal that you're armed unless you intend to use the gun, and believe me, I intended to if that thing came out at me. I pulled the gun out and casually held it, barrel pointed at the ground. I know the thing saw it, cause it immediately turned away from me where I could no longer see its eyes, but I knew it was still there.

I decided I needed to get out of there. Being a church, the grounds were fairly large and there weren't any houses nearby. I was pretty much out there alone. I started slowly walking back towards the residential part of town. I could always bang on someone's door if this thing came after me.

I tried not to turn and look to see if it was following me, but I couldn't help it. I didn't see anything. I then remembered how I'd vowed to take back my life and not be afraid, and I got mad again.

I turned around and shouted out to it, "You bastard, I don't know who you are, but if you don't leave me alone you'll have hell to pay." I was mad.

I then heard the most mournful sound. It was low and almost sounded like a growl, getting higher and ending in a kind of crying sound. I knew then that this wasn't something that was a part of my world. Where it came from I didn't know, but I knew it was a wild thing and didn't belong here in town. Why was it here? Was it living in the thicket, kind of lost, just like me?

I was terrified, but I managed to remember what my dad had always told me, that there's a logical explanation for everything. I'm not a superstitious person, and I have my dad to thank for that, because every time I was scared of something as a kid, he'd make me sit down with him and analyze it and figure it out. He also helped me understand how the human mind can see patterns where there really aren't any and turn them into spooks and such.

But I knew this thing was real cause it was now following me again, and it didn't seem to be as cautious or afraid of being seen. It was just right there, next to that house in the shadows, I could see its eyes glowing red—and its outline—which was massive. It was definitely real. But what was it?

Did it intend to try to harm me? I realized my little pistol wouldn't even make a dent in a creature that large. I decided to just go on back to the office and see what it would do. I slowly walked back, and the fear seemed to be a bit less, or I was managing to control it better.

I got to the office, unlocked the front door and went in, glad the burger joint was still open and there were people over there. It would close in about a half-hour.

I decided to listen to some music, something I hadn't been doing because I was afraid of being caught camping there. I turned on my little radio and cranked it up. An old Patsy Cline tune was on:

I've been out walkin', after midnight, along the highway, just searching for you...

I started laughing—there couldn't be a better song to describe my night. For some reason, I was no longer afraid. Maybe I just didn't care any more.

Before long, the burger joint's neon lights were off and I was alone on Main, except for the Robber's Hideaway down the street a bit. But I no longer felt lonesome.

I cracked open a book and tried to read, but my mind was too distracted, wondering what was outside, and what the creature was doing.

"Hell, I just don't care anymore," I said out loud to myself and went outside, standing by the front door. I remembered my brother once telling me that I was the only one who had the power to change my life.

Just then, right on cue, a police cruiser drove by. I watched as he turned around and came back, slowing down, then stopping.

"Everything OK, Sir?" he asked.

"You bet, Officer," I replied.

"Good, good, you have a nice night." He turned back around and continued on down the street, leaving me shaking my head at my own paranoia.

Nobody cared if I was living in my own building, and as long as I didn't do anything to make someone complain, I'd be OK here. I didn't need to sneak around. I went back inside and put up the tarps and went to bed, radio still on, slowly drifting into a deep and restful sleep.

I know that some people believe you can influence things with your mind, but I'm a pragmatist and I don't really believe it. But I do think that your attitude is picked up in subtle ways by others, and I think that's what happened with me and the creature, cause after that night, I never saw it again. I think it somehow noticed that it wasn't dealing with a victim any more.

My entire attitude changed, and I began to look more at what was right with my life. For now, I had shelter, and everything would soon work its way out, and I knew I would eventually get a home again. I knew this because I would make it happen. Human intention is a very powerful thing.

I continued going for my walks, and I never felt like I was being watched again, even when I went over by the church. I eventually lost that paunch and felt better from the exercise and started taking off at lunch and walking then, too.

Pretty soon, I was on a new bicycle I'd bought, and before long, I was riding in bike marathons for charity and all that. I made a lot of new friends that way.

My wife and I divorced, and she got the house, but she also got the house payments. That freed me to get a nice little apartment. I decided to sell the office and just work from home, and that cash gave me a nice buffer.

I no longer walk at night, as I instead ride my bike every afternoon and then work some in the evenings. But once in awhile I'm in the area by the thicket and I wonder just what that thing I saw was, and what its intentions had been.

I guess I'll never know. I do know that fear is one of humankind's most powerful emotions, and I never want to live that way again. In a way, I have that creature to thank for making me aware of that.

[12] Mexican Mountain Madness

Jay was quite the guy to have along on a fishing trip. He made everything a lot of fun, and I was sure his wife could hear us partying clear over at their place in Utah, even though we were on the upper White River in Colorado.

He had a non-stop energy, even though he was an old codger, and he outfished us all. He also out-ate us all, out-partied us all, and even out-snored us all. So, when he told this story, I was surprised at the dark tenor of it, coming from him. It must have been quite the experience, to say the least.

My name is Jay, and I used to be called the Bluejay of the Canyons because of my little blue Cessna. I inherited it from my dad, who was one of the early pioneers of canyon aviation. He flew many a uranium miner in to find that elusive strike, and then he would fly them supplies and what not. He learned to fly from his dad, and he knew that country like the back of his hand.

I guess I know that country pretty well, too, as I've been flying it since I was a kid. I soloed when I was 16, the youngest they would let you.

I mention all this so you know that the experience I'm about to relate was unique. I don't think my dad or my granddad could top my tale, and they had some good ones.

I was a pilot for many years for Eagle Aviation, a flying service that did about anything you needed a plane for. We had offices and planes in several towns in southeast Utah. I owned it with my brother, who was also a pilot. We sold it and retired a few years ago.

One of our bigger areas for business was the Moab region. We flew a lot of sightseers around over the canyons, and that was the majority of our business there. I was pretty much the one who ran that office, and my brother ran the office in Price, Utah. He'd had his fill of tourists and would rather fly the oil and gas guys around. His hangers were also where we'd take the planes for servicing and that kind of thing.

Well, I'd been having some minor problems with a little Piper Cub we had, so I decided to take it on up to Price, which is a short jaunt for a plane, about 100 miles from Moab. I'd have my brother Lenny take a look at it with his mechanic. I could fly something else back down, then go swap planes when it was fixed.

I got up to Price, no problems, and headed back to Moab in another little Cessna they had swapped me. The thing flew just fine. I had no problems of any kind with it at all, not until I got about halfway, that is, then it started acting up. I was just over the lip of the Wedge, if you know where that is. Yeah, I know it's not really on the way from Price to Moab—I was doing a little sightseeing over the Swell. Those canyons are something else.

Years ago, before I took over the Moab office. We tried to run an office out of Green River, but we just never could make a go of it. We'd fly tourists over the Swell, but the place just wasn't known enough.

I would even fly people in to the old historic uranium boom airstrips, the couple that were still left, which was quite a thrill. There were two we could legally use, Mexican Mountain and Hidden Splendor. I could land both strips with my eyes closed, which is saying a lot.

Anyway, like I said, I was over the Wedge, which is that point where people go to look down into what the tourism board calls the Little Grand Canyon. I have never heard anyone else call it that, they all just call it the view of the San Rafael River from the Wedge. It is quite a sight, though, and there's even an arch visible, if you know where to look.

It's fun to come over it in a light plane, because there's always a downdraft, and you can give your passengers a little thrill when they feel the bottom fall out from under them.

I was enjoying my flight back when all of a sudden I hit that downdraft. No problem, I'd hit it many times before, and I knew how to work it, but this time, that little plane started down and I couldn't get it to come back up. It acted like it was stalling.

I've experienced every kind of stall you can, flying in those canyons with their unpredictable air currents, but I couldn't get this little plane to respond.

Now I was pretty much going down, and I didn't like the feel of that one bit. I was right smack in the middle of some of the most tortured country on the planet, and believe me, there was no place to land anywhere.

I managed to think clearly enough to get on the radio.

"Mayday, mayday, this is Bluejay, coming down by the Wedge in the San Rafael. Mayday, mayday."

I then kind of floated down into the San Rafael drainage, which is a good thousand feet below the rim of the Wedge. But I got my engine back, and made some altitude, flying right by Bottleneck Peak. Then I lost power again.

I was beginning to suspect a fuel line problem, given the sporadic nature of things. Not something I could fix way out here alone. But I'd worry about that bridge when I crossed it and hopefully landed.

I thought that maybe I could come down on the Mexican Mountain road, which was pretty bumpy and primitive, but I'd done it before. It was late autumn, and I didn't figure there would be anyone out in this wild country, which would be good for landing, but bad for getting help.

I had banked a bit and was cruising along the road, only maybe 60 feet above it, getting ready to land, when I saw the darndest thing. Someone was walking down the middle of the road, someone big and all dressed in brown.

I aborted the landing and managed to get enough fuel going to get some altitude back, thank God. Whoever that was, it would've destroyed both it and the plane if I'd hit it.

As I flew back up, I caught a glimpse of a face that I must have immediately blanked out. I could only deal with so much right then.

I was now back at about 200 feet, not even close to being high enough to clear the big cliffs of Mexican Mountain quickly coming up right smack in my way. Just on the other side was the City of Stone, a landscape sculpted from white rocks and as wild as it gets.

If I could get enough altitude to clear Mexican Mountain and manage to cruise over the City of Stone, I was home free, because all there was after that was flat Mancos shale desert, and the Green River airport was close.

It was not to be. I tried to get going, but things were getting bad again, I was losing altitude. I could see the San Rafael River in the near distance, and then the flanks of the mountain. I couldn't see any place to land at this point, the landscape was rugged cliffs and rock outcroppings.

I knew that the Mexican Mountain airstrip, what there was of it, was just down a ways, right next to the river and over that small hill right there, but I needed a bit more juice to get there, I wasn't quite on it. I pulled back the throttle and lo and behold, power returned.

Dare I try to climb and cross Mexican Mountain? If I turned back and tried for more altitude and circled and then tried to climb over it, I would have no place to go if I lost power again.

I decided to try for the airstrip, it seemed to be my only realistic hope. I banked a little, afraid to do much in case I lost power and stalled. I managed to get headed in the direction of the little strip, and I knew it wasn't far.

My odds were good, if I could just get set up for the landing, as I had no second chance. There would be no aborting the landing and trying again. I had better make good the first time, and the San Rafael River was right at the end of the strip, so I better set down exactly where I needed to.

I followed the road, maybe a mere 50 feet above it, then came to the area where it ended at a small parking area. This was at the top of a hill, and I then banked on down into the river drainage and the airstrip.

I could see it coming up fast, and I banked a bit more, turning into the cliffs right behind it. You didn't have much leeway when landing here, and only pilots with back country experience better even try it. And only a fool would try it with the river at the bottom of the run, not the top. But I had no choice.

The airstrip used to be maintained by a backcountry pilot group that would drive in, hike down there, and pull weeds and remove rocks that had fallen from the cliffs.

These backcountry strips were just bare dirt. Most of us didn't use the strip any more, it was just too big of a liability taking people in there, too dangerous, so I had no idea if the strip was being maintained or not, though I was hoping it was. I would soon know.

The BLM wanted to shut these old airstrips down, especially this one, since it was in a wilderness area, and maintaining the strips gave the pilots a right to keep them grandfathered in, since the strips were here long before the BLM. I was hoping it was still being cleared.

The strip was coming up fast, and a good thing, because my engine had now totally stalled. It acted like it was getting no fuel at all now.

I had managed to get it right on track for the landing, but I was a little high. It would be tricky, I had to come down exactly right. This strip was notorious, only a good bush pilot could land it.

I started dropping fast. The cliffs were on my left wing, nearly touching. The best way to land this was from the other direction, as the strip was a bit uphill and that would slow you down. It wasn't a long strip.

And coming in that way, if you didn't stop in time you just ran into the scrub, not the river. I was coming in all ass-backwards, but it was my only chance, and I was glad for it. And now I could see that the strip hadn't been maintained. Tumbleweeds were waist high all the way down it. That could prove to be a problem.

I felt the weeds grabbing at the wheels. I was going way too fast, and bounced back up into the air, then hit again. I had my foot as far into the brakes as you could get, and I needed to stop right now, the river was coming up fast.

I bounced some more, hitting my head on the ceiling and biting my tongue. I could now taste blood, but of more concern was the river—I was almost in it.

I had to think fast, and I decided the scrub to my right would be better than the river, would give me a bit more of a chance, and though there would be a jolt, I had slowed enough that I might make it.

I turned hard to my right and ran off the strip, but the weeds had wrapped around my wheels and axle, and I was now bound up in a juniper tree, bringing me to an instant stop. I heard a snapping metal noise, felt my neck pop, managed to turn off the engine, and all was quiet.

I thought I was seriously injured, the way my neck had popped, but as I sat there, I gently moved my head a bit and found I seemed to be OK. No pain.

I hoped that someone had picked up my mayday and that my emergency beacon had received enough of a jolt to go off, which would hopefully bring help. I would need it. The nearest highway was over 40 miles away.

I needed to get out of the plane, but the door was stuck shut, and I was tipped forward so much I kept sliding into the windshield. I managed to twist around so I could kick at the door hard enough that it popped open, and I tumbled out, slumping to the ground.

I just sat there for the longest time, trying to feel if I were injured and assess my situation. My tongue was sore where I had bitten it, and my left arm hurt from the jolting, but I felt OK otherwise. I was worried I might have whiplash, but if so, it didn't hurt and didn't seem to incapacitate me any.

I finally stood up and looked around. The plane was nose down in a grove of juniper trees, the front wheel completely wrenched off and the wreckage of a sheared tree all over the ground. The right wing had pushed into the trees, tearing off the metal skin and the tip of the wing.

No way would anyone fly this thing out, it would probably sit out here forever. I hoped my brother had insurance on it.

I sat back down under a tree. It was a nice cool autumn day, and this was bad, because it meant the night would be cold, and I had no survival gear of any kind.

I always carried survival gear—a sleeping bag, water, food, but I had forgot to transfer it from the other plane. It would be a long cold night if someone didn't come after me. I didn't even have any matches or a lighter to start a fire. I was up the river, so to speak. I decided I needed to plan now for the night and what to do. I needed water, too.

The river was right below me, but the San Rafael is a slow deep muddy river with thick tamarisk all along its sheer banks, so getting to it wouldn't be easy, and I had nothing to put water in.

I looked around. There was plenty of wood, but I had nothing to light it with. Maybe I could stay in the plane, but the way it was tipped meant that was a no go. I couldn't sleep with my face jammed into the windshield.

Damn, I hoped someone was out looking for me. I knew my brother would get a search party going if he hadn't heard from me by evening, but that would still mean I had to spend the night out here.

OK, I had to sit back and think about all this, remember that I had just survived a plane accident, the pilot's worst nightmare, and that I was OK and should be appreciative to be alive. A couple of my buddies hadn't been so lucky. Someone would find me. Not to panic. Just take it easy, hang out, get prepared for night the best you can, and wait.

I'm an impatient person, it's hard for me to wait. And I know now I was in shock. That's just how something like that is, even if you're not injured, you go into shock, mentally if not physically.

It finally occurred to me to climb back into the plane and see if the radio was working. God almighty, it was! I called out and immediately got another pilot.

He must be going right over me, and sure enough, I could see a contrail above—it was a big 747. I gave him my location and he said he would call it in, then he was gone.

I waited, trying to get someone else, did the mayday thing again, waited, did it again, waited, but no one else came on. I then decided to look around the cockpit, as much as I could, to see if there was an emergency kit somewhere.

No kit, but there was a blanket on the back seat, and I grabbed that up. And glory be, I found a lighter on the floor, which was good luck for me. We never allowed smoking on a plane, so I wondered where it had come from. Maybe some tourist had dropped it. I tried it out, and it was empty. So much for the good luck.

I tried the radio again. Nobody. I crawled out of the plane and decided it might be prudent to make some kind of shelter for the night. I found a small depression under a big juniper that was filled with juniper needles that had fallen through the years from the tree.

I kicked the area out a bit so it was a little deeper, then kicked more detritus from the tree into the depression. This would be my bed, I would hunker down here with the blanket and at least have a comfortable place. But I'd been out camping many times, and I knew it would be a long miserable night without any heat.

Now I could hear a plane in the distance! I got out onto the strip and waited so it would see me, then decided to run over and try the radio. All I got was static, so I ran back over to the strip.

Someone appeared to be crisscrossing the sky, and I knew it was a search plane. I waited on the strip, but they never came this way. They seemed to be more concerned with searching over by where I had called out my first mayday, over by the Wedge. Damn.

Now the sound was gone. "Come back!" I yelled out, but nobody did. I felt deflated. It was now getting on to late afternoon.

I went back to my juniper bed. I decided to try to bank something around it to keep any breezes out. How in the heck did the Fremont Indians survive out here many years ago? They knew how to start fires, I thought. Maybe I should figure that out.

I found a couple of rocks and tried scratching one across the other to get a spark. No luck. I decided you needed something besides sandstone to create a spark with. I looked around the plane, maybe there was something there.

I searched the plane some more and found a book of matches behind the seat. I couldn't believe my luck, much better than an empty lighter. I gathered some small twigs and juniper bark and soon had a small fire going.

Hot damn! I was smokin' now! But I needed to keep this thing going. I doubted I would be so lucky twice in a row, as I had only a few matches left. I looked around and found a big dead juniper and managed to drag it over to the fire.

Careful now, I thought, if you drop it in the middle of the fire, you're likely to just put the fire out. So I dragged the tree up next to the small fire, added more dried-out juniper bark, and watched the fire spread into the tree. It started burning with great gusto, being all dried out. It had probably lay there dead for a hundred years.

Now I had a pretty good bonfire going, and it was getting on to dusk. I needed to get a wood cache that would last me through the night. I would just sit here all night by the fire, or maybe I could even get a bit of sleep, if I could find some big logs that would keep burning. No way I wanted that fire to go out.

I hiked around and found some more dead trees, dragging them back next to my fire. This was a lot of work, but it got my mind off everything, and it meant survival. I must've spent an hour gathering wood, and now that plane was back! I knew they had seen the smoke.

I remembered a guy who had got lost over in Canyonlands National Park at the Island in the Sky and had done the same thing I was doing. He intentionally set a few trees on fire so the smoke would bring someone to him, as nobody knew he was lost. It worked great, he was rescued, but he also got fined by the park service for the fires. Typical government, I thought.

If they fine me, fine. They could fine away, I was just trying to survive. This was a wilderness area, so I doubted if anyone would really worry about it anyway.

Now the search plane was almost above me! I ran out to the strip and waved my arms. They would see the wreck first, but hopefully they would then see me and know I was alive and come in for an immediate rescue.

They saw me! They waggled their wings, and I ran for the radio, climbing into the tipped cockpit.

It was a plane out of Green River. They wanted to land on the airstrip, but I had to advise them against coming in, against my own wishes. We didn't need two plane wrecks out here.

"Jay, are you OK?"

"Pretty much," I answered, "But I sure don't want to spend the night out here."

"Can you start walking down the road? We just called the Emery County Sheriff, and they're on their way. Can you start walking and meet them? It may take them a few hours to get there. That road is washed out in a couple of places, and it would mean a quicker rescue for you."

I almost said yes, then something flashed across my mind, something I had completely repressed. I didn't need it along with my other troubles, so I'd conveniently forgotten all about it.

It was that big brown thing walking on the road. Oh my God, where was it now? A cold shiver went down my spine.

"No way I can walk that road at night, fellas," I backtracked. "I don't have a light of any kind. Just send the sheriff in, they can find me at the strip. I'll keep the fire going. If you have any water or something to drink, though, could you drop it off?"

"Roger," the pilot answered and banked back around me, barely skimming the cliffs. They were soon overhead again, and something tumbled out of the plane, landing on the runway.

I ran out and picked it up from the weeds, taking a moment to find it. It was an emergency kit! It had matches, a space blanket for warmth, some MREs and candy bars, a small flashlight, and some fruit drinks for energy.

I jumped for joy, giving them the thumbs up, but the plane was gone into the dusk, over Mexican Mountain, back to Green River.

Now I went back to tending my fire, which had really taken on a life of its own in my absence. You know how a fire is after it's been burning awhile, it gets a nice hot bed of embers going and really puts out the heat. And juniper wood burns nice, has a nice smell, too.

I pulled a log over next to the fire and had a candy bar and some fruit drink. That really picked me up, and my spirits were much better now, knowing I would soon be rescued. I noticed my neck was getting a bit sore.

Now I could relax a bit, and I realized I'd been running on sheer willpower. I knew I was kind of in shock. I slumped down a bit off the log and, leaning against it, went to sleep.

I had a bizarre dream where something big and brown was trying to get me, where I was stumbling in the dark and managed to get inside the plane, and now it was rocking the plane from side to side, and I was tipped forward in the cockpit yelling at it, blood running from a cut in my forehead where it had lifted the plane up and slid me into the window, tipping the plane on its side. It was a horrible nightmare, and I woke, moaning, terrified.

For a moment I thought I was in the plane, but then I realized I was by the fire. There was something wet and sticky on my hands, and I thought I'd spilled fruit drink on them.

The fire had crept up the entire length of the tree and the whole juniper was ablaze, lighting the night sky, crackling and popping embers into the air above me. I felt spent, I could do no more, but I had to get up and see what was going on.

The wood I had piled for the night was close to being ignited, and I needed to get around to the other side of the tree and drag it away. I wondered when the sheriff would get here. I needed help, I was exhausted.

I managed to stumble around the burning tree and began dragging the logs and limbs I'd collected away, where
the fire couldn't reach them.

I was dragging a big log and dropped it and stood up
straight, feeling dizzy. I then realized I was looking directly
into two blazing eyes. I thought they were reflecting the
glow of the fire, they were so red. They were a good eight or
nine feet off the ground, and they were swaying from side
to side, like a ghost in the wind.

I turned and quickly got back on the other side of the
burning tree, putting it between me and whatever it was,
chilled, in spite of the hot fire just a few feet from me. The
eyes stayed put, swaying, watching through the flames.

If I hadn't seen the creature before I'd crashed the
plane, I would've thought I was hallucinating from shock,
but I knew better. This was the creature I'd dreamed about,
that had trapped me in the plane and tried to get me.

It was a bit much on top of surviving a plane crash to
now have to deal with some night monster. I sank down
and started crying from fear and exhaustion.

I must have passed out, because the next thing I remember was waking up with the sensation of being on fire.
I jumped up and sure enough, my boots were smoldering,
the soles were hot from the fire's heat.

I started stomping into the ground, as my feet were getting really hot. I then quickly pulled the boots off and let
them cool down before putting them back on. The smell of
rubber was nauseating.

My God, what next? There was more, but not at all more
of what I expected. I knew it had to be past midnight from

the way the Big Dipper was tipped in the sky, and still no sheriff.

I could now see a glow behind me, where the plane was, and I turned to see it was on fire! It wasn't even near the big log, an ember must have started it. No way, I thought, how could an ember start a metal plane on fire?

There wasn't much I could do but stand there and watch it burn and wonder what I would tell my brother, if I survived all this. And then I noticed it was tipped onto its side. Then it dawned on me—maybe the beast had set the plane on fire. How else could I account for it?

The plane was really blazing now, and I came to my senses—the fuel tank would blow up when it caught fire, and I was in danger. I was too close. But I wanted to stay by the fire as protection from the creature. What could I do?

I had to get away from the plane, no matter what. I grabbed my emergency kit, turned on the flashlight, then thought to grab a thick stick from the edge of the fire, which would serve as a torch.

I managed to stumble away from the plane to the landing strip, where I turned and watched the entire thing explode, just like in the movies, pieces of metal and debris flying through the air. It was pretty impressive.

And now I could see, in the light of all this, the brown beast running as fast as it could, away from the explosion, and straight towards me!

I ran to the far edge of the airstrip, where I hunkered down behind a small rock outcropping and waited. I turned off the flashlight, and the torch lit up everything around me. I just crouched there and waited.

Now the creature began bellowing like a mad bull, and it was still coming my way! I panicked. I reached over with the torch and set the weeds in front of me on fire. There was nothing flammable behind me that I could see, just desert, so if I could keep a fire between me and the creature, maybe it would go away or even burn up.

At this point, I decided I was in complete shock and hallucinating, maybe I even had a brain injury, the way my neck had popped. Strangely enough, this took the fear away, and I began feeling like a general in a field campaign, planning strategy and all that.

I would burn the SOB out. If the fire spread, I would back my way down to the river for safety. I would burn this whole wilderness up if I had to. I would win this battle. I started thinking of some of the war movies I'd seen as a kid and really got into it. I had no fear at all, just pure manic energy.

Things went crazy. The entire strip, which was just a big patch of dry tumbleweeds, caught on fire. The plane was still burning, and now my big wood pile over by the old juniper log was burning. All I could hear was a roaring sound, the kind that fire makes when the wind whips it to a fury. It looked like the entire world was on fire, but I knew the tumbleweeds would burn off fast. I turned and ran towards the river.

As I inched my way off the bank into the icy cold water, I heard the roar of the fire behind me. Hot ashes floated towards me, and now the tamarisk along the river bank were looking like they might catch, huge embers landing in their branches. The smoke got thicker and thicker, and I started coughing as my lungs began to feel like they were burning up.

I started laughing, coughing, laughing again. The stress of the entire event had been incredible. I had managed to survive a plane crash in some of the most remote wilderness in Utah, then decided I would probably instead die of hypothermia from the cold, but then a rescue looked likely, getting my hopes back up, but instead I'd had to defend myself from what looked like an angry Bigfoot, and now it looked like I might die of smoke inhalation.

But the tamarisk didn't catch, and soon the strip had burned clean. The air currents turned, and the smoke went away, and I could make out the juniper logs burning over by what appeared to be black smoke floating up from the wreckage of the plane.

I had to get back over there, I was getting really really cold. The water had soaked me through and through. I decided to make a run for it, beast or no beast.

I worked my way over to the fire in the darkness, afraid to turn my light on and reveal where I was. After later reading a lot about Bigfoot, I discovered that my light was about the only defense I had, as they have excellent night vision and hate light. But I didn't know that at the time.

I made it over to the juniper fire OK, stumbling a bit, and I was soon basking in the warmth. Where was the beast? I was delirious, I think, because I shouted out, "Come on over and get warm, you SOB! Bring some marshmallows!" I did this over and over, shouting into the darkness.

I nearly jumped out of my skin when I heard honking from up the hill on the road. The sheriff! They were finally here! I was ecstatic, but almost afraid I was hearing things. I no longer trusted my senses.

I started crazily yelling, 'Over here, over here, over here!" And I was still yelling that, delirious, when they finally got to me, a good half-hour or more later. I was afraid to leave the fire, so I waited for them to come to me. The road ended a good half-mile away, so it took them awhile.

I don't remember much, except them cleaning blood off me from the cut on my head, and then someone asking how the hell could anyone survive that explosion, and it was a good thing I hadn't been caught in the resulting wildfire.

It was dawn by the time we were back on the Mexican Mountain Road, heading for Green River, smoke rising behind us in the distance. I heard later that the tamarisk had indeed caught fire and burned a good mile or so on down the river.

I wondered if the BLM would send me a bill, but everyone thought the plane had started the fire, plus tammies are invasive and a pest and the government's been trying to get rid of them ever since they invaded the riverways, so I figured I did them a favor. Maybe I would send them a bill.

But I hadn't started that fire, it had been started by the plane. My weed fire on the runway had quickly burned itself out, and the juniper logs weren't going anywhere. It was the plane fire that had thrown embers and debris into the tammies. And after finding that the cut on my head was real and not a dream, I knew who had started that fire.

I hope he got away and didn't burn up. I have no idea why he had it out for me, but I wish him no harm. Maybe he didn't like airplanes. I just never want to meet up with him again.

But he did manage to make sure I stayed warm and didn't die of hypothermia, which was nice of him.

[13] The Bigfoot Drive-Through

I love Montana, and lots of great Sasquatch stories come from that wild and unpopulated state. The following was kind of a humorous one, though Barry, the storyteller, said it really wasn't very funny when he had his first and only Bigfoot sighting—he was scared to death. But he has that way of telling it that often comes from doing newspaper feature stories, and he made it all a lot of fun. I hope to be up there next year for their annual Bigfoot Barbecue.

Big Hole, Montana, is a nice little spot by the road, though there isn't much there. Most of the townspeople like it that way, and a lot of them retired there to get away from the city. The town never changes much, and the newspaper died out years ago from a lack of news, which is exactly how everyone likes it.

But there were a couple of weeks a few years ago that things were different. The newspaper was still around, and they had a major heyday reporting on the events.

A couple of outside reporters also come to town, and even one from the big town of Bozeman showed up. I'm Barry, and that big town reporter was me.

It all started out with a call from one of my colleagues, Lacy, a fellow reporter over in the major leagues of Helena, who called and asked if I'd heard about the going-ons in Big Hole. I said of course not, nobody ever heard anything about the going-ons in Big Hole, because there never were any going-ons in Big Hole.

I asked her to clue me in, and she said there had apparently been a monster sighted on the outskirts of town, and it had been harassing people. It started out with a woman seeing a black creature stealing a pie from her windowsill.

I wasn't even aware that people still baked pies and let them cool on windowsills, but my friend assured me we were dealing with Big Hole, where anything from the past was quite possible.

I kind of laughed, telling Lacy she had the wrong number, this was the *Bozeman News*, not the *National Enquirer* or *Star*. She said I was missing out on a good story because now things had escalated, and she was going down there herself to check into it. Apparently a number of townspeople had seen the creature, including the mayor and the one and only newspaper reporter. These people were all of good character.

She had talked to the reporter herself, and they were starting to think they were being hoaxed. She had decided to go cover it for two reasons: one, things were slow, and two, a good hoax is hard to come by. I should come down and get involved in the fun, and by the way, had I ever heard of how good the fishing was in the Big Hole River?

Things were a bit slow in Bozeman right then. Most of the university students were gone, since it was summer, and there hadn't been any grizzly bear incidents. The buffalo in nearby Yellowstone were behaving and not charging tourists, and yes, I had indeed heard of the fishing in the Big Hole. I needed a few days off, and if I could come back with a good human interest story, all for the better. I was on my way.

I pulled into the little town of Big Hole that evening, hoping to get a motel, but soon realizing that wasn't likely to happen. There was only one motel there—it had eight rooms, and they were all full, no vacancy. I suspected that the town was having a run on reporters, which would boost their annual tourist revenue. I wondered if this wasn't a plot by the tourism board to do exactly that.

Sure enough, not one plate on the cars at the motel was local, but then, locals typically don't stay in local motels. So I guess my efforts as a sleuth weren't going to get me far.

But I did notice one car from Helena, and I figured that had to be Lacy, so I knocked on the room's door. Sure enough, it was her, and she was even glad to see me. Like the crack reporter she is, she had beat me there.

We went and talked to the motel proprietor, who had a little camp trailer he said I could rent for the price of a room, though it had no plumbing, but I could come in and use the bathroom at the office.

So there I was, set up in a seedy little camp trailer behind the Pillow Talk Motel, paying the same rate as those who got to enjoy the full amenities. But at least is was private and quiet.

Lacy and I decided to go get some dinner, and we ended up in the local greasy spoon, the Squat and Gobble. As we sat there, we could hear the people next to us talking, so, like good reporters, we eavesdropped.

They were discussing the latest encounter, a new one just as of a couple of hours ago. But they first had to give a synopsis of what had happened to date, starting with that first encounter with the woman seeing the thing steal her pie right off her windowsill.

The sheriff had come out and taken the report, but he forgot to look for tracks (he wasn't really used to this kind of thing), so she called him back the next day after she had found a number of big tracks, and he tried to cast them.

The next night, a fourteen-year-old girl had called in and reported a huge dark creature looking in her window as she was watching TV. She had run and locked herself and her dog in the bedroom, scared stiff.

The dog had been acting strange all evening, its hackles up, trying to get her to go upstairs, pushing on her and then sitting by her on the couch and growling.

She had stayed hidden until her parents came home. They hadn't really believed her until the next day, when the pie story was all over town, and then they decided to call the sheriff, who came out and very authoritatively looked for and found more tracks. Big tracks, a good 18 inches long and twice as wide as the sheriff's foot, pushing deep into the hard ground, just like at the pie woman's house.

It was beginning to seem like the whole town was being terrorized by this creature, and the incidents had now escalated to about two or three a night. The latest incident, the one we overheard at the next table, involved the mayor himself.

He had heard his dogs whining out in the yard late in the evening and gone out to check, when he saw a huge beast stripping his raspberry bushes. He quickly brought the dogs into the house and called the sheriff.

The sheriff, who was by this time sleep-deprived and exhausted, deputized the mayor right there on the phone and told him to investigate it. This didn't set too well with the mayor, but there wasn't much he could do, since he had driven the police cruiser home that night, as his wife needed to go to a piano recital and needed the family car.

The mayor investigated the incident by taking his shotgun out back and firing buckshot into the bushes, though he suspected the thing was long gone by then.

The story tellers at the next table found this incident somewhat humorous, and repeated it when a friend came and sat down with them, so we got to double check our notes.

While we were having dinner, another incident was in progress, though we didn't know it, just across the street at the local pizza drive-through. This little place was all decorated with flags that flapped in the wind, and it had the best pizza in town. It had one of those ovens where you put the pizza in one end on little rollers and it rolled through the oven, coming out perfect every time.

They had just finished cooking two large pizzas, pepperoni and double cheese, when the waitress saw someone walk up to the drive-through window.

She opened it to take their order, saw a large hairy man standing there (she reported it as being at least 12 feet tall), threw the pizzas at him, and ran off, screaming. When the owner and cook came over to check it out, there was no man and no pizzas.

When the sheriff came to investigate the next morning (having to wait until then as the mayor had his cruiser), about all he said was that it was probably a big waste to throw pizzas at it.

At this point, the entire town was in a flurry. The local paper had printed a story in that week's paper called, "Bigfoot Terrorizes Big Hole." It didn't really have anything new, everyone had heard it all through the grapevine. It did report, however, that the paparazzi had hit town, meaning us, of course. It also reported that a lot of people wanted to see a big hole in the Big Hole Bigfoot.

The mayor decided to convene a meeting of townspeople to assess the situation and see if anyone had any ideas on how to deal with the problem. Quite a few people showed up, at least for Big Hole.

Right in the middle of the meeting, the sheriff got a call on his radio, and there had just been another incident at the drive-through. The Bigfoot had tried for more pizza, but instead, got run off with a couple of fish sandwiches thrown in its face.

The sheriff rescheduled the meeting for the next night, then went out to investigate, looking frustrated and tired. I was starting to feel kind of sorry for the guy.

That incident was followed by a couple of hunters sighting the creature on the edge of town, sitting on the road bank, eating something. They were afraid to shoot at it, thinking it could be a guy in a gorilla suit or something.

That night, I had my own incident. I woke up to an earthquake. I knew it had to be an earthquake, as the little camp trailer was shaking from side to side so hard I thought it might actually tip onto its side.

I jumped up and ran outside, just in time to see the creature. I didn't see much of it, but I did see enough to see how massive it was. It wasn't just tall, it was huge. That made me a believer, and I no longer believed it was a hoax.

It was about 2 a.m., and I decided it was my duty to call the sheriff and wake him up. But the mayor was still deputized, and I got him instead, as the sheriff was instead getting a good night's sleep. The mayor's eyes looked red, but maybe it was from the flashing lights on the police cruiser. He went over and turned them off, then came inside.

We needed to talk, he said. Since I was from the city and had a bit more experience with these things, maybe I could help him figure out how to get rid of this problem, the Big Hole Bigfoot, as it was now being called. I told the mayor that I didn't have any advice, as I didn't have a clue what to do.

But after we sat there for awhile, I did have some advice, which was simple. They needed to quit feeding this thing and make it have bad associations with the town.

I had experience with habituated animals, covering stories about people feeding black bears and deer and such, and it seemed to me that this Big Hole Bigfoot was becoming habituated to the town and associating it with food. That needed to change. Even if the feedings were accidental, they were still feeding it.

How could they change that, the mayor wondered. I didn't know, but finally, a plan formed in my sleep-deprived mind. Why not make lots of food available to the creature, but make the food bad, so bad that it would decide to go elsewhere?

We decided to sleep on it, and the mayor went home. There was no way I was going to sleep in that little trailer after the Bigfootquake, so I ended up in my car. Not much protection if the Bigfoot returned, but at least I could turn the ignition key and leave.

The next morning, I had a call from the mayor asking me to join him for coffee at Karen's Slo Mo Cafe. I think the idea behind the place was that the mo coffee you drink, the mo slo you go, weighted down with that bad stuff, so she could then sell you lunch.

The mayor wanted me to let him know how we could solve the problem of the Big Hole Bigfoot. I told him we had been through all this the previous night, and I had given him the only suggestion I knew. He was impatient, saying he knew that, but how could we make the town un-palatable to the creature?

I repeated, "Make the food bad. This Bigfoot is getting habituated to good food, make it bad. You know, red peppers, jalapenos, mustard, that kind of thing."

He looked excited, and said, "You're a reporter, write this down!" I wrote "jalapenos, red peppers, mustard" on a napkin and handed it to him and then asked him where the best holes in the Big Hole were.

I hadn't had a chance to go fishing in the Big Hole River yet, and I was really hoping to do so soon. Montana's rivers are famous for their warm waters that breed fabulous trout.

A lot of this is due to the hot springs that keep the waters warm. The rivers are also wide and shallow, making them easy to wade and get to the holes where the big fish hide.

This Bigfoot story was getting bigger and bigger and was taking a lot of my time to cover. I knew this would be my last day here—I needed to get home. Lacy had left yesterday. I wanted to fish the Big Hole.

I'm not much of a serious fisherman—I actually just like to be around the river, and carrying a rod is a good excuse to do so. I waded out into the water, finally enjoying myself, the real reason I'd gone down there.

I'd heard people talk about the Big Hole for years, and it certainly was living up to its reputation. There were a couple of other fishermen down the river a bit, but I basically had this whole stretch of the river to myself. And it was a beautiful sunny Montana summer day.

I had just hooked a fish that felt like it weighed at least five pounds, when I caught a glimpse of something in the bushes on the other side of the river. I couldn't remember if Big Hole had moose, but that's what I thought it must be. It was big and brown.

If it were a moose, I was leaving. I had been charged by one up on the Gallatin, and I was basically terrified of them. They were big and not a bit afraid of humans and could do a lot of damage. I had covered more than one moose-charges-human story, and the moose rarely got the bad end of the deal.

My attention went back to the fish. I had definitely caught something bigger than anything I'd ever caught before. I tried reeling it in while keeping an eye out for the moose.

Just then, I saw the thing in the bushes again, and it wasn't a moose, it was a grizzly. Much worse than a moose, but not a Bigfoot, at least, as I'd been half expecting that, too.

OK, a grizzly, and I have a big fish on the end of my expensive Ross Reel. Should I go for the fish and for keeping my reel, or should I get out as fast as I can and get to the car? What would you have done?

Just like you probably would have, I dropped the reel and waded that river as fast as I could, looking behind me all the way as that grizzly walked into the water. My reel had caught in the rocks, and the fish was flapping in the water, making a real fuss. The grizzly walked right over to it and caught it, eating it right then and there. He hadn't read the rules about catch and release.

By then, I was on the other side of the river hoofing it as fast as I could to my car. I realized I hadn't even taken a photo, and it would make a good story. Oh well. That reel only cost a mere $400.

Back in town, I went to my motel room, the one Lacy had vacated, and caught my breath. That was as close as I wanted to get to a grizzly, and now I'd had encounters with both a wild bear and a wild primate, if that's what the Bigfoot really was.

I went into town. The townspeople had outdone themselves with their cooking, and everyone had set out jalapeno pies, hot mustard burgers, and red pepper pizzas on their window sills and backyard picnic tables. The plan had been executed.

That night, the Bigfoot chose the drive-through again, and they were ready. When the owner saw that black head peering though the drive-through window, he opened the side door and threw out two pizzas, hot from the oven and piled high with jalapenos. The Bigfoot grabbed them and ran off, and I bet it regretted not ordering a cold drink to go with them. That was the last Big Hole Bigfoot encounter. Where it went, nobody knows.

Two weeks later, I received a news clipping in the mail from the mayor. They had established an annual Big Hole Bigfoot Barbecue, which featured hot and spicy foods.

He thanked me in his short note, and offered to buy me a cup of coffee if I was ever in town again. I must admit I was a bit disappointed, hoping at the very least for a pizza.

[14] The Revelation

This story was one of the most poignant I've heard, and I can't say it's a fun story. It's actually kind of heartbreaking, really. But it shows how character can determine our actions.

The man who told it was every bit as nice as he portrayed his uncle as being, so I guess it runs in the family. He was part of a group from his company who was spending a week fishing the upper Yampa River.

This story kind of haunts me, I guess. I sure don't want to see what he saw, I know that. And the thought of a huge Bigfoot drinking a little cup of tea really boggles my mind. I wonder if he held his little pinkie up while drinking it.

My Uncle Ted was the sweetest old guy you could ever meet. He really was my great-uncle, but we just called him Uncle Ted. He was a retired minister, and he had spent most of his life helping people. Even after he retired, he helped everyone out. Sometimes it was financially, more often emotionally or in dealing with problems.

He met my aunt when she was just 17. He was a sailor, quite a bit older than her, maybe in his mid-20s, and boy did her parents discourage that relationship.

They married when she was 18, and a more dedicated husband you could never ask for. After he got out of the Navy, he went to what they called Bible School, and he became a minister.

They had a good marriage, and it lasted over 50 years. After my aunt passed away from heart problems, he was broken hearted. I don't think he ever recovered. He mourned her and missed her terribly. They had always been together, they did everything together.

We all felt so bad for him, and my mom tried to get him to move in with us, but he wouldn't. He didn't want to be a bother. He wouldn't have been a bother, we all enjoyed his company. We wanted to return some of the good he'd done for us and others, but he wanted to stay in his own home. I really didn't blame him, but we knew he got terribly lonely.

He was in his early 80s when my aunt died. They were always out and about, doing things, and now he became a complete homebody. We couldn't get him to go anywhere with us.

But one day, while my mom and I were over visiting him, taking him some home-cooked food, my mom, who drives the van for the senior center and is always all over town picking people up, remarked that she'd heard from someone that there was a destitute old man living in the bushes out by the power plant.

Some kids had seen his camp, and it was a big mass of leaves and twigs, a big nest. And he had a bunch of string tied all over the trees, and what looked like a couple of big walking sticks. No one had actually seen him, but once in awhile one of the kids would be riding their bikes by there and they would get an eerie weird feeling.

One time, they got a quick glimpse of the guy. He was very tall and had silver hair. They knew he lived there, and he must be very poor. He also was in bad need of a shower, as the place smelled kind of rank.

This was right up my uncle's alley. He had lost his will to live, but all of a sudden he became very interested in this vagabond guy. I think it was a case of identification, that's all. My uncle felt sorry for this lonely old guy because he himself was a lonely old guy.

My uncle told me later that he had driven over there and scoped it all out, hoping to see the old man. I think it was the first time he'd mentioned going anywhere for many months. I kind of worried about this, as I didn't know what was up, and I sure didn't want anything bad to happen to Uncle Ted.

I talked to my mom about it, and she then talked to Uncle Ted and made him promise to not go over there alone again. I found out later that he continued going over there, but he took his little terrier dog after that so he wouldn't break his promise and be alone.

He started going over there about every day, according to his neighbor who I later talked to about it. She saw him leave every morning and head that direction, so I assume that's what was going on. She actually asked him one day what was up, as she also wanted to keep an eye on him, as we all did.

He told her he was going out for a drive each day, as it made him feel better. When she flat out asked him where he drove to, he said he always started over by the power plant, where he had begun taking a sack of groceries to the old homeless man every day.

Sometimes he even took him hot cups of tea, he told her. The cups would be returned each day to the drop-off spot, so he knew the guy was enjoying the hot drinks. Sometimes the old guy would leave him gifts, things like pretty rocks and carved sticks.

The neighbor called my mom, and my mom lit into Uncle Ted, but in a nice way. She talked to him about being alone out there with a complete stranger, and did he have a clue what that old guy was all about? What if he came and knocked him on the head and stole his car or something?

Uncle Ted just sat there sheepishly and said that if the guy wanted his car that bad, he could have it. My mom threw up her hands and fumed and fussed and ended it all by pleading with my uncle to be very careful. He assured her he would.

Well, one blow after another, his little dog died of kidney failure. Now my uncle truly was alone, and he was very attached to that dog. We all worried about what effect this would have on him, and we tried to get him to adopt another dog, but he wouldn't. He said it wouldn't be fair to the dog to have an old guy like him as an owner, especially since he knew he was going to die soon.

This really made my blood run cold. How could he know that? Was he suicidal?

We intensified our contact with him. My dad now got involved and went over there every day to check on him, and my mom would call him every evening and talk for awhile to try and cheer him up. We were always taking him baked goods and casseroles and things like that, but I was suspecting they were going to the old homeless guy.

One day after school, I rode my bike over to Uncle Ted's, as I did occasionally, just to say hello. I finally got up the nerve to ask him what he meant by what he'd said.

He told me that he had a bad heart, and he knew he was going to just keel over one of these days. He hadn't meant anything morbid by it, and he encouraged me to not worry, that death was a part of life, and he was ready.

He then told me, "But I know it won't be for awhile. I want that old guy out there to reveal himself before I die. I want to talk to him and get to know him, see if I can help him out."

Just like Uncle Ted. Postponing his own death to help someone else.

So, he kept going out there every morning, leaving food. I think he was becoming a bit obsessed with it. It had given his life the only meaning it seemed to have, and he craved that. He started going out there in the evenings, sometimes not coming home until well after dark.

The neighbor spy reported back to my mom on all this, and Mom was livid. She told him, "It's bad enough for you to be hobnobbing with a complete stranger who very well could be a mental case, but for you to go out there at night is totally unacceptable. Don't you care that we worry about you?"

Of course he did, and he said he would stop coming home after dark. From now on, he would be home by late evening at the worst case. And he was true to his word, according to the neighbor spy.

The days wore on, and the old guy refused to reveal himself to Uncle Ted, who had taken to leaving books and even a Bible. These disappeared, so he assumed the old guy was reading them.

He also left a couple of L.L. Bean catalogs with a note that indicated he would buy him whatever he needed, just to mark them and tell him the size. The old guy never did. All he seemed interested in was the food. Oh, and a sleeping bag Uncle Ted left him, with a couple of pillows.

Through all this, the old guy would leave presents, like the rocks and sticks.

Uncle Ted then told me he didn't think the guy could read and write, and he sure wanted to help him. He started leaving pictures each day with simple words that associated with the picture.

For example, he would leave a picture of an apple with the word "apple" written on it. He would leave paper and a pen for the guy to use and hopefully write notes back, but he never did.

But one day, Uncle Ted found a dead dove lying in the exchange spot. He was horrified and didn't know what to make of it, especially a dove, the symbol of peace and the Holy Spirit. So he left it. It disturbed him, thinking the old guy had killed it.

My uncle refused the gift. He wasn't sure what effect this would have on their relationship, what there was of one. He actually didn't go back out there for a couple of days, but then he got to worrying that the guy would be hungry.

My mom found out and sent my dad to talk to him. He told Uncle Ted he wanted him to move in with us, and if he refused, we would make a case for his mental stability and force the issue. It was the only way my parents knew to safeguard the old guy. This upset Ted a lot, I know it did.

Uncle Ted had now begun leaving notes for the old guy. Dad found one in his car after it was all over, and it basically was begging the old guy to reveal himself so they could talk. Uncle Ted said he knew he could help the guy find a home and peace, if only he would reveal who he was and talk. This theme was repeated several times.

One evening, about eight p.m., my mom got a call from the neighbor spy. Uncle Ted's car wasn't home, and she hadn't seen him since early afternoon. We'd better come over.

My parents went to his house, but there were no signs of anything, no problems. My mom called the police and sent them out to the old power plant. I think she knew something was terribly wrong and couldn't deal with finding my uncle.

She was right. The police found him sitting in his car, hunched over the steering wheel, dead.

On the windshield was a note, stuck under the wiper. It was illegible. Whoever wrote it had no idea what coherent handwriting was, it just looked like scribbling. Next to it was a shiny silver cross my uncle must have given the old guy. I knew the old guy had left it there, maybe after my uncle died. Maybe it was my imagination, but it seemed to have a sadness to it.

The autopsy said Uncle Ted had died of a heart attack.

Later, after it was all said and done, my mom asked me what I thought had happened.

I simply said, "Mom, Uncle Ted finally had the revelation he'd been wanting, but I don't think he saw what he expected to see."

"What do you mean?" she asked.

"I think what he was dealing with wasn't human at all, and when he realized that, it scared him and he had a heart attack."

She just nodded her head and started crying.

[15] Bigfoot Cassidy and the Great Train Crash

There are lots of great Bigfoot stories from the Pacific Northwest, which is actually more or less the birthplace of the Sasquatch legend in the U.S. And on another note, I bet there were lots of great stories the railroad hobos of the 1930s could tell.

But to combine the two—well, I'll let you read it for yourself. It's a great tale, told around a campfire right in my own backyard by a good friend's nephew.

I'll tell this story on behalf of my grandpa, who told it to me many years ago. He swore it was true, and I actually checked the newspaper for that time and sure enough, there was a train wreck exactly like he had told about, except they left out one part, the part about what caused it.

I guess it was just too outlandish for them to expect anyone to believe, and they had their reputation as a newspaper to worry about. Or maybe they just didn't know. But my grandpa told the story just a tad differently, and he was there.

My grandpa was a travelin' man, he used to ride the rails. He was young and wanted to see the country, and it was the only way you could do that if you were poor, which he was. Back then, in the 1930s, a lot of guys traveled this way. Nobody had any money, it was during the Great Depression. My dad's family is all from Klamath Falls, Oregon, and that's where my great-grandparents lived.

My grandpa was in his early 20s when all this happened, but he was still pretty much living at home, when he was around, that is. I know his parents worried about him—probably with good reason, as I think he was pretty wild.

He loved trains. Later, he became a train engineer, that's how much he loved them, and he loved trains until he died. I think that when he was young he was going for train rides just to be on the trains, not to travel.

When he died, he left a huge collection of train memorabilia to a train museum in Colorado, where he had moved when he started his train career. I think maybe after this incident he didn't want to be on the trains in Oregon much.

I have to digress here for a moment and tell you about my grandpa's little dog, Hobo. She was a beagle, and he taught her what the word "train" meant.

After he retired, he lived not too far from the tracks so he could see his beloved trains, and that crazy dog would sit there and listen for them, then go bezerk, baying and whining, until the train came by, then she would sit there pointing at it with her paw, like she was telling Grandpa to look. She could hear the trains coming long before the rest of us, and he called her his train detective.

Everyone always got a kick out of that silly dog. Grandpa actually took her on a train once, but I don't know if she made the connection or not. She probably did, as she was smart as a whip. It was something else hearing her baying at the trains. Actually, Grandpa took me on a train a number of times, and I'm now a train engineer, too.

Along that line, Grandpa used to teach me railroad songs when I was just a little kid, and I'll never forget one that just epitomizes what he was doing back then. I don't recall all the words, but they go something like:

Chugga chugga chugga on down the road,

Chugga chugga chugga with a heavy load.

Sittin' in a lonely boxcar, boys, followin' a cannonball.

Anyway, back to the story. Grandpa was riding this empty train up somewhere in central or northern Oregon. I don't recall what line it was, and he and a couple of other railroad bums were holed up in a boxcar, trying to stay warm and out of the wind.

He said it was about mid-train, and it wasn't a real big train that day, maybe 25 cars and two engines. Not huge, but sizable enough. The cars were all empty, so the train was making good time, flowing through the Oregon forests in the black night.

These other two guys he was riding with, he'd met them somewhere or other, but they weren't really friends, just acquaintances, which is how it usually was, riding the rails. You'd meet someone, ride along together for awhile, then your paths would diverge, and maybe you'd meet them again someday, maybe not.

Some of the guys were real rough characters, but some were just young men trying to make their way someplace new or get away from everything. Some were alcoholics, some sober as the day is long. You'd just meet all types.

These guys were all holed up in this car, and it was the middle of the night. They were just chugging along, following that cannonball, trying to sleep, even though it was winter and cold. This being Oregon, they were in the middle of a big forest, and a light snow was falling.

My grandpa didn't really care for the company he was keeping, so he couldn't sleep. He didn't trust them and thought they might rob him or worse, even though he only had about five bucks to his name.

So, he was sitting there, kind of nodding off, then waking up again from the cold. A boxcar isn't the best digs one hopes for in the winter. It's a miracle they didn't all freeze to death, as that did occasionally happen.

He heard the lonesome whistle blow, and the train started slowing down. This was kind of odd, cause they were out in the middle of nowhere. There must be something on the track. He crawled up to the top of the car, but it was too dang cold to stay up there long, and he didn't see anything but steam coming from the engine, which was normal.

He slumped back down into the car, and the other two guys slept. Now the train was slowing even more, and he didn't know what to make of it. The cars were bumping against each other like trains do when they come to a stop, and the brakes were squealing.

Now, all of a sudden, the train was speeding up again. Just then, they went through a very dark tunnel. He wondered if something wasn't in that tunnel and the engineer didn't want to hit it. Maybe a moose or something.

Now the train was back up to full speed, and now it was slowing again. What the heck was going on?

He crawled up to the top of the car again, but this time what he saw gave him the chills. Something big and black was walking along the top of the train, balancing on the tops of the cars like it was nothing.

Only a monkey could do something like this, he thought, and whatever it was did look a bit monkey-like, even though it was way way bigger than any monkey.

He slumped back down into the car. What in the world was he supposed to think? A big gorilla, walking along the top of the train, precariously balanced on the cars? He must be dreaming. Should he wake the other guys up to verify if he was crazy or not?

He decided not. They were better off sleeping, and he was likewise better off with them sleeping. There was something about the pair that he didn't like. The train continued to slow.

My grandpa knew now that something was wrong, the engineer was having some kind of problems. But there wasn't anything he could do about it, slumped down in a big boxcar halfway back the train.

He crawled back up to take a look and almost got stepped on by yet another gorilla thing. He was right smack behind it, so it didn't see him. He about had a heart attack. The thing walked on down the train cars like it was walking down a flat level street, nary a worry about falling off the moving train.

Now, my grandpa started thinking maybe it was time to abandon ship while the train was still going slow. He would be stranded out in the middle of the forest in the winter, who knows how far from civilization, but maybe he could hop the next train that came through. The thing that worried him was what if there were more of these creatures out in the forest, and he went from the frying pan to the fire?

He'd heard tales from other hobos about traveling through Oregon and Washington, tales with characters just like these gorilla things. He had thought they were the result of too much alcohol, but maybe they were real.

His hobo companions just slept through it all. They must be warmer than he was or full of whiskey, he figured.

The train slowed almost to a stop, and he decided it was time. He crawled to the open door and jumped.

He landed on the edge of the railroad berm, rolling on down into what ended up being a ditch full of weeds and snow. Remember, this is a young and very agile young man. If I tried to do something like that, I would probably break something.

The train rolled slowly on and was soon gone. All was silent. The snow had stopped falling, and my grandpa now wondered if he'd done the right thing. He made his way over into the edge of the forest, hiding. He would sit it out, try to stay warm until dawn.

Maybe another train would roll through and he could wave it down, though that was unlikely, as these engineers usually weren't too happy about giving out free rides. But a man out in the middle of the forest might be different.

Then he remembered how it could sometimes take these big trains a mile or more to stop. He would have to slow one down somehow and hop on. He had no idea how that would work.

He sat there in the cold, wondering if he was crazy to have jumped off that train, when he noticed two black figures not too far from him, kind of doing the same thing, standing in the edge of the forest.

A chill came over him. He knew it was the gorilla things. He now wished he hadn't jumped, as it appeared they had also. He was scared to death and just stood there, hoping they wouldn't notice him.

But now he was getting stiff from the cold. He had to do something, either start a fire or walk around and try to stay warm. If he didn't, he would freeze. He was already starting to shiver, the first sign of hypothermia. He wondered how long it would be until dawn.

Now he heard something the likes of which he never heard before or since. It sounded like it was miles away, a huge crashing noise, the sound of grinding and metal twisting and, above it all, a shrieking. The train! It had wrecked! And it sounded like it had been really moving along! He was now glad he'd jumped.

He could now hear someone talking in the distance, and he realized it was the two forms he'd spied. They must be humans! He decided to go see, even though he was very nervous about it.

He decided to skirt the forest, kind of staying behind the trees a bit so they wouldn't see him. It didn't take him long to get near them, and sure enough, there were two men standing there, talking quietly. He sure didn't want to hook up with his companions again, so he stood there awhile, watching and listening, making sure it wasn't them before revealing himself.

He stepped out of the forest and quietly said, "Hello, fellas. Sounds like that train just bit the dust. Were you on it?"

The two guys were shocked to see him, jumping back a bit. "Where the hell did you come from?" one asked. He told them, and come to find out, they were the engineer and brakeman. They had purposely slowed the train down enough so they themselves could jump.

My grandpa was shocked, to say the least. A good crew never abandoned the train. But he knew why, they didn't even need to tell him.

They built a big fire and stayed close to it until dawn. My grandpa got the story from them that cold night in that Oregon forest, and it was a story he barely believed himself, even though he had been there and seen the creatures. He found himself shivering again, even though he was standing by the warm fire.

Seems the engineer had seen something on the tracks, something big, and had slowed down to not hit it, sounding the whistle. The thing has stepped aside just as they were nearly on it, and the engineer about had a heart attack when he saw what it was.

He thought he saw the beast reach out and grab the rail on the side of the engine, pulling itself up onto the train, just a they entered the tunnel. This gave him the cold chills, and he radioed the brakeman, who quickly came up.

They discussed what he'd seen, and the brakeman decided to take a look, going to the side of the engine and stepping out onto the catwalk. He came face to face with the thing, and he himself about had a heart attack.

He jumped back in, slamming the door and bracing it, then ran back to the engineer with his report, who then informed him he'd seen a second one on board. It had actually leaned down from the top of the engine and peered into the window at him.

The engineer now put the train into high gear, thinking maybe a good bit of speed would knock the things off or they wouldn't be able to hold on. He thought about radioing in and telling Dispatch what was going on, then decided he didn't need to lose his job, as they would think he was drinking.

Now the one beast was hanging off the side of the engine, trying to break in through the side door, and it sounded like another up on top. They needed a plan, but all they could think of was to somehow abandon the train without the beasts knowing, letting the whole thing roll on down the line. They knew it would eventually crash with no one manning the brakes. But they had to get off before these things broke in.

The brakeman now came up with an idea. He would go to the second engine and open the door, then quickly run back to the first engine. This would hopefully divert the beasts while the two men bailed out the side door. But they needed to slow the train enough to make an exit.

The engineer got on his radio and sent out a message that the train was out of control and they were going to jump, with an approximate location. They needed someone to come find them, he said.

Soon they had the train slowed down, and the brakeman went to the back engine and opened the door, yelling out to the wind. He ran to the first engine, and they both jumped into the night, hoping they were unseen. Apparently the Bigfoot hadn't seen them jump, and the train rolled on down the line to its demise.

We were rescued the next day by an engine pulling a caboose with a rescue crew. It had to push the caboose back the way they came, as the tracks weren't passable ahead, from the big train wreck.

My grandpa quit riding the rails after that, which made his parents very happy. He said he always wondered what happened to the two characters in the boxcar there with him.

[16] Runaway Bigfoot Ramp

I once saw what a friend called a runaway hikers ramp, which was a big sandy strip that had just naturally formed on the steep downside of a hiking trail. We thought that was kind of funny, but this story takes the idea into a new dimension.

I found this account fascinating, and the next time I was on the pass, I found the ramp. It truly has been the site of numerous accidents, and the cars' occupants have always, to date, survived.

Have you ever driven Red Mountain Pass, over by Ouray, Colorado? If not, consider yourself lucky. I grew up near there, and the first time I drove it, I was 16 and had barely had my driver's license more than a month or two.

My sister had a friend, Sue, who needed a car brought up from Farmington, New Mexico, and she was willing to pay me $100 to do it. That was a lot of money for a kid, especially doing something most adults wouldn't let them do. All I can figure is that my sister's friend was desperate.

It was a weekend in late May, and Sue and I took off for Farmington. Sue owned a small used-car dealership, and

I think she was one savvy gal, because she was living in a nice house and had a nice RV and all that. I think she knew how to buy and sell used cars.

We got to Farmington, and I found out the car was a big Lincoln Continental. That thing was huge to someone who had driven only a VW Bug until then (my sister's).

By the time we'd had a bite to eat and done the paperwork, it was dusk. We left Farmington, Sue following me in her small car. I later wondered why we hadn't swapped vehicles, since she was the experienced driver. I later found out—she was afraid to drive it over the pass.

It took me awhile to get to where I was even confident enough to drive that big fancy boat slowly down the road. I had to practice a bit in a big empty lot first. I'm tall, but I still had trouble seeing over the front of the thing, it was so darned long. But we finally took off, and by now it was dark. I just steered it down the highway between the center and side lines, hoping for the best.

The road on up to Durango, Colorado from Farmington isn't bad, and I soon had adapted and relaxed a bit. We stopped for gas in Durango, and I got a cup of coffee and tried to relax even more.

I knew what was coming up—three miserable steep and scary Colorado passes—Molas Divide, Coalbank Hill, and then Red Mountain Pass. I'd been over them all, but had never driven even one of them. The creme de la creme was Red Mountain, a pass so scary that even the locals would go the long way around if they could. By long way around, I mean a route that added a good 60 or more miles, clear down through Slickrock and Dove Creek, or maybe over Lizard Head Pass.

I was getting nervous, but Molas and Coalbank weren't too bad, there wasn't much traffic, and since it was dark I couldn't see off the edge and tell how scary it was, though I already knew. I tried to just focus on the road.

We got down into Silverton around 9 p.m., and I wasn't tired yet, though my eyes were a bit strained from trying to make sure I stayed right smack on the center line, at least until another car came, then I would get over. We stopped to get out and walk around a bit at the visitor center there, which was closed, then headed on out.

Going up the Silverton side of Red Moauntain Pass wasn't too bad. There are a couple of switchbacks, but they're fairly gentle and the curves aren't too sharp.

I was nearly on the top of the pass, and I was amazed at the power this car had. If I weren't careful, I could easily be going a good 20 or 30 miles an hour faster than I thought I was. I had zipped right up that pass, and I noticed Sue was lagging a bit behind in her underpowered little car.

I slowed down at the top, because you'd better, or you're history. That's where the switchbacks really start. The minute you get to the top and start down the west side, you're greeted by a switchback so sharp you think you're going to get dizzy and lose control before it's all over. I'm really not exaggerating.

But that's just the beginning, because it doesn't really get exposed for a bit. After a few miles, you not only have narrow steep switchbacks, but you can now see a good thousand foot drop off the side, sometimes off both sides. It's not for the faint of heart.

I slowed way down, so much so that Sue was soon on my tail, her lights blinding me, which made things much worse. I must've been taking those switchbacks at 15 m.p.h. or less. I was scared stiff.

I couldn't really make out the side of the road very well, as the highway needed a new paint job, and that big Lincoln felt like it was hanging out over the edge at every sharp curve. And then there was Sue, riding my tail.

I finally got down to a place where the pass flattens out into a high meadow for a couple of miles, and I pulled over. Sue pulled over behind me. We were the only cars I had seen on the pass, as it was late.

I got out and stretched, then told her I thought she would be wise to drive the big car the rest of the way. We should now swap. She reminded me that I was getting paid to do this, and I needed to carry on. I then realized she was white-knuckled and even more scared than I was. That was why she was tailgating me.

OK, I said, but you have to lead. She didn't want to do this, but I told her she was blinding me, and I was going to lose it when we got to the next bad part of the pass, which was worse than anything we'd been on yet. So she reluctantly agreed to lead.

Off we went, Sue in the lead, going even slower than before, which was OK by me. Before long, we were at the really scary part of the pass. Of course, we were just prolonging the agony by going so slow.

Red Mountain Pass is narrow, and to make things worse, there aren't any guardrails on most of it. This is for good reason—if there were guardrails, the snowplows couldn't plow the road, it's that narrow.

Many a lost soul has gone over the edge at various places on the pass, especially in winter. This includes a few unlucky snowplow operators, taken to a cold icy death by avalanches.

The pass has over 200 snowslide areas along its route, and keeping it clear of avalanche danger is a major project in the winter. The pass is periodically closed for avalanche control, which means setting off mortar shells, and then plowing the avalanche snow and debris off the road.

By the time we came though, there was no avalanche danger, but the lack of guardrails was just as disturbing as in the winter.

Sue continued on as we passed under the snowshed that had been built at the famous Riverside Slide after it took a number of lives, including those of a minister and his two daughters on their way to church in Silverton. This is where the pass began in earnest as far as I was concerned, because this is where the extreme exposure began.

I tried not to notice. I knew what was there, or rather, not there, and it scared me to death in that big boat. All I could do was grit my teeth and follow Sue's tail lights.

Or not, because she was going off the road now, straight over the side. I stopped, watching her slow-moving tail-lights disappear straight over the side of the cliff.

There really wasn't any place to park off the road, but I inched the big boat up as close to the inside cliffs as I could, then fumbled a bit until I found the emergency flashers and jumped out.

In case you haven't guessed by now, I'm terrified of heights, and just getting close enough to the edge to look over in the dark took a lot of courage. I inched my way over, feeling sick.

I could see her taillights still, going slowly down, which made no sense at all. It looked like she was driving down the side of a huge ramp at about 15 m.p.h., not falling and tumbling, as one would expect. I stood there and watched until her car finally came to a stop, far far below. I could tell in the dark it was still upright.

Just then, someone was at my side, and I noticed another car parked behind mine. A man stood there, then asked what was going on. I told him my friend had just gone over the side. He said he would go on down to Ouray and get help. I should stay where I was so they could find where the car went down in the dark.

I never felt so alone as when that guy drove off, leaving me standing there by the side of the road above that gaping canyon. I could still make out Sue's tail lights far below.

I have no idea why, but I yelled out, "Turn off your lights and save the battery so you can drive it home." I have no idea what I was thinking, there was no way that car would be in good enough shape to drive home.

I was shocked to hear her yelling back, but I couldn't make out what she was saying, it was too far away. It had to be Sue, and that was good. She was at least able to yell, so maybe she wasn't injured too badly.

I yelled back, "Help is coming, help is coming." I thought I heard a distant "OK."

As I stood there, looking down with nothing but starlight to shine the way, I thought I could see something coming up that steep ramp. I was scared and didn't know what to think, but it looked like a dark form was just kind of floating up.

I hurried back and got in the car, locking the doors. The night air was chilly, and I knew it would be awhile before help arrived. There was nothing I could do.

I thought another car had stopped because someone was standing by my window. But just then, another car came by, stopped, and whatever it was ran off.

"Everything OK?" someone asked. I was too stunned to remember much, but before long, Ouray County Search and Rescue was there, along with an ambulance. They set up a big spotlight and roped down to the car. Sitting inside, still stunned but unharmed, was Sue. She had survived a 400 foot drop. Even stranger, her car had survived a 400 foot drop. It had only a couple of small dents where it had hit rocks.

Later, after being admitted to the hospital for observation, Sue was released the next morning, after making sure she wasn't in shock and was OK. She got her car from the wrecker and drove it home. Nobody could believe the car wasn't damaged.

My cousin Gene is on the search and rescue team for the county, and I later asked him about it. He said that she was incredibly lucky, because in most of the canyon, the cliffs just dropped straight into the valley floor, a thousand feet down in places.

But this particular place had a huge granite ramp that had eroded out, going right from the highway to the bottom. It was a steep angle, but not a cliff. He likened it to a downhill runaway truck ramp.

It was a bad curve, and they had rescued a family in a van from the same place last winter, and again no one was injured. But what he didn't understand was why Sue didn't go down faster and hit the bottom with a bang.

The van that wrecked had been slowed down by deep snow, as it went off the side in the winter. But there was no snow now, just rock, and Sue should have gone down faster.

After I talked to Sue later, she told me that it felt like something had grabbed onto her car and just held it back all the way down. In fact, she said that was why she ran off the road, she had seen something big and black standing there, and it had surprised her, and she had taken her eyes off the road.

As she passed it down the steep incline, she said it felt like it grabbed her bumper and slowly walked that car down to the bottom.

I believed her, and I told her I too had seen it, after her car had landed and while I was looking down there. I had seen it come up the incline.

She sighed and thanked me for helping her confirm she wasn't going insane, then handed me two one-hundred dollar bills. She said I might need the extra for therapy.

I forgot to tell her that I had talked one of the rescuers into driving the Lincoln on into town. But I figured it didn't matter.

[17] The Back Forty

I've saved this story for last simply because I really like it, kind of like you save the really good wine for after dinner. And though the location is kept under wraps for obvious reasons, I will say that it took place in the state of Arkansas, which has had a number of Bigfoot sightings and even a couple of tales of habituations.

The story was told over a campfire deep in prime Bigfoot country—Colorado's Flattop Mountains.

When I was in the sixth grade, I had a friend called Wasp. Why he was called Wasp, I have no idea, but that was his name, Wasp Jensen. Wasp was kind of a tall gangly kid, and he had red hair that stuck out all over. It seemed like he never combed it, or if he did, it had a mind of its own.

Wasp and I weren't friends initially, as he came into school mid-grade and was kind of quiet and shy at first. But after a few weeks, he kind of got his stride, and he became just the opposite.

Wasp started telling everyone all about himself, anything you wanted to know was game, and he was the complete opposite of shy. I think he was just assessing the situation at first.

Wasp lived out on a ranch, he told us, a few miles out of town, and he and his mom were what he called "loners." I found out later that he meant something different by that word than what I though it meant, he meant he and his mom were all alone out there. Apparently his dad had left them, and thus, they were loners.

Looking back, I think Wasp was kind of a genius and none of us recognized it for what it was. We just thought he was odd. He definitely didn't have many social skills, and some of the teachers had a hard time with this.

Wasp would just blurt out anything in the middle of class, things like what he'd had for breakfast (or more likely, the fact that he hadn't had any breakfast), how he had to ride the bus from now on because their car wasn't running too good, that kind of thing, just out of nowhere.

He actually acted like he'd never been in a school setting before, and I found out later that the sixth grade was his first introduction to education. He was totally home schooled, and by that, I mean he taught himself stuff while his mom worked, leaving him home alone. He had never even had a teacher.

Given all that, he was amazingly knowledgeable. He knew more math than the rest of us put together, could read better, and asked smarter questions. That's why I think maybe he was a genius.

The kids pretty much steered clear of Wasp because he was different, and because he was poor. His clothes were clean, but worn and out of style. He didn't have a television, so he had no clue what the latest TV talk was about.

He didn't even have any way to listen to music, so he was out of it there, too. I think the lack of these things made him develop his intellect more, which turned out to be better in the long run, but he definitely didn't fit in.

I took a liking to him, probably because I was always kind of the class geek, as I liked scientific stuff. Wasp seemed to be knowledgeable about anything I could throw at him. He had built a Van de Graaff generator. He knew how to make a radio from a few wires. He could build stuff from nothing. And he understood the physics behind it, something I hadn't grasped yet.

So Wasp and I got to be friends. One day in class, while Mr. Ramsey, our history teacher, was discussing the Anasazi Indians, Wasp blurted out, "I think there might be oil on our ranch. We'll make a lot of money if there is."

Mr. Ramsey patiently asked Wasp to save it for after class, when he could tell us more about it. Wasp looked hurt.

I asked him after class about the oil, and he said his mom had some guys coming out that very day to discuss buying the mineral rights from her. I knew they were desperately poor and this was a big deal to Wasp, so I let him talk about it until the bus showed up, then he got on it, and I walked on home.

The next day, I asked him about the oil business and he said that nothing had come of it. He also asked if he could share my lunch, as his mom had forgot to pack him one.

I knew they didn't have any food, so I talked to Mr. Ramsey between classes. He got Wasp on the free school lunch program that very day.

Wasp and I had gotten to where we spent our lunch time together, planning or working on science stuff. We were right in the thick of designing a nuclear power plant. Wasp said he thought if we could do that, we could get a lot of power going and sell it and get rich. Wasp was always trying to come up with get-rich schemes, and I knew it was because he was so poor, so I would go along with them.

One day, Wasp didn't seem to have any interest in the nuclear plant, even though I'd managed to get a book on one and we had now sketched it out on paper and every-thing. He seemed distracted.

That afternoon, he blurted out in Mr. Ramsey's class, "We got a new family living on the ranch now."

Mr. Ramsey said that was nice, and went on talking about the Incan Indians. I think Wasp felt comfortable in Mr. Ramsey's class, as this was the only class he would blurt stuff out in. Plus, it was history, which I knew he found boring, and I think his mind would wander, and he would forget where he was and just blurt whatever out.

I asked Wasp about the new family after class.

"Yeah, we have an old school bus out on the ranch down in the willows, and a family has moved into it. There's a mom, a dad, and a kid. They're ugly."

I thought it was odd that someone would move into an old school bus way out on Wasp's ranch, but times were hard, and I let it go.

The next day, Wasp reported in Mr. Ramsey's class that his mom was helping the family out and giving them food, and he was worried, because they really didn't have enough food to just give it away, and these guys ate too much. Mr. Ramsey asked Wasp to come see him after class. Wasp turned red. He knew he was in trouble.

But he wasn't, not really. He reported back to me that Mr. Ramsey had given him a lecture about talking in class, but had seemed more concerned about the food situation and wondered if he was getting enough to eat.

Wasp had replied, "Well, Sir, all you have to do is look at how scrawny I am and know the answer to that question."

Mr. Ramsey talked to the school principal, who took the matter up with Wasp's mom, who reported back that they were having hard times, but she had just managed to get onto food stamps, so things were looking up. She said that yes, she was helping some others out, but all they were getting was scraps, and she was also getting them road-kill off the highway.

The principal made a secret deal with the school cook to slip some of the leftover food from each day's school lunch into Wasp's book pack. I think Wasp had most of it eaten before he got home each day.

Wasp started growing like a weed. He'd been tall and gangly before, and now he was even taller and ganglier. But he was growing, and that was good. It meant he was getting the nutrition he needed. He was actually becoming a very nice looking kid, my mom said, after she saw him and me talking at the bus stop.

One day, in Mr. Ramsey's class, Wasp once again broke in and informed everyone, "That family I told you about, they're getting scary. Oops, sorry, Mr. Ramsey, didn't mean to interrupt."

Mr. Ramsey smiled and said it was OK, and could Wasp again please see him after class.

Mr. Ramsey was concerned about what Wasp had reported and wanted more information. Why was the new family scary? Wasp said they were scary because they were big and ugly and were now starting to come up to the house wanting food, and his mom was giving it to them. This concerned Mr. Ramsey, but he wasn't sure what to do.

I, of course, heard all about it at the bus stop, where I hung out with Wasp each day while he waited for the bus. Why were they scary? Why was his mom feeding them? I wanted to know more. Wasp said I should come out on Saturday and visit and see for myself.

This was the first time Wasp had invited me to the ranch, and I was pleased by that, yet a bit nervous about this "ugly family" situation. I decided it would be OK, but no way was I going to spend the night.

The next Saturday, my mom took me out to the ranch. We had a bit of trouble finding it, as it turned out to be off a road no longer maintained by the county and the sign was down, but we finally pulled off a bouncy dusty dirt road into his driveway, such that it was. Wasp stood there grinning at us.

The ranch was really more of a junkyard. Wasp and his mom lived in a small two-bedroom trailer that was so faded it was hard to tell it had once been yellow. The little wooden porch was tippy and the hand rail had long broken off.

Wasp's mom came out to meet us, and she was a pleasant woman who looked like she might've once been a beauty contest winner who had since come on hard times. Her face was drawn and tired looking. She had beautiful shoulder-length blonde hair that was naturally thick and curly, but her eyes were tired looking. She said hello and welcomed us to the ranch.

I instantly liked her, and so did my mom. They ended up talking for a long time, while Wasp and I went out to explore the ranch.

"This here's the Back Forty," he pointed to a bunch of old abandoned rusted-out cars. "There's forty of them there. And there's the Back Twenty." He pointed towards more old cars by some cottonwoods that appeared to flank a small creek.

"It isn't much of a ranch, but my Grandpa gave it to us. He died a few months ago. Before this, we were living in that old school bus that the new family now lives in."

He pointed down past the cottonwoods, and I could make out the top of something. I walked over to the side of the road to get a better look.

"We had it parked over in Coalville, and we moved it here when we got this place. My mom set it down by the creek for a getaway place, but that was before the family moved in."

"Can we go down there?" I asked, not really wanting to.

"Nope. Well, yes, I guess you could, but I'm not going with you, and you might never come back."

I studied his face to see if he was kidding. He wasn't.

"Let's get back over to the house," he added. "That ugly bunch has ruined this place for me."

Just then, I could see something moving down there. It was big, and it made the school bus look like a VW Bus, it was that big in comparison. A strange feeling came over me, and I wanted to turn and run.

I suddenly wanted to go home. "Say, Wasp, why don't we go back to my house? My mom's still there, talking to your mom, and she can bring you home later."

"I can't leave my mom here alone," he replied. "Now you understand what I was talking about in Mr. Ramsey's class. It's dangerous here. He thought I was joking, but I wasn't. It's OK when I go to school, as my mom's at work then, but I can't leave her here alone. That's why I never attend anything on the weekends at school or go to anyone's house. This place is getting creepier and creepier, and I don't blame you for wanting to go home. My mom's bleeding heart is to blame. Maybe another time, huh?"

I felt really guilty, but I had to leave. I thought I was going to be physically ill. I told my mom I was going home with her, as I didn't feel very good all of a sudden. It was the truth. Wasp's mom looked like she knew what was going on. She looked a bit sad.

We left, and I wondered if I should tell my mom. I was worried for Wasp's safety, as well as his mom's. I decided my mom wouldn't believe me, so I said nothing.

But as soon as I got home, I called Mr. Ramsey. Maybe he would believe me. But when he answered the phone, I chickened out and hung up.

I spent the rest of the weekend worrying about Wasp and his mom, out on their ranch. I knew now that his announcements in class were his way of trying to deal with the pressure he was under. He was begging for help the only way he knew.

The next Monday, I was happy to see Wasp get off the bus. Later, he announced in class, "Mr. Ramsey, I hate to say anything and I know I'm interrupting class, but we have some researchers coming out to our ranch."

By now, Mr. Ramsey was pretty much used to Wasp's ways. He just nodded and said, "That's nice, Wasp," and continued talking about the Aztecs. After class, I asked Wasp about the researchers.

"My mom's still feeding that family, and this guy found out, and he's a researcher and wants out come out and see them."

I asked Wasp how he felt about that. He answered, "I don't care, cause they'll just disappear. They won't let anyone but me and my mom see them. You got a look only because they didn't know you were around, but usually they come up only at night, and we don't even really see them very often, which is OK by me, they're so ugly. They can research away all they want."

The next day, I was eager to know how the researcher thing went, and I met Wasp as he got off the bus. He looked tired.

He reported that two guys had shown up and set up these little remote cameras all over the place, then they had set out some really nice turkey and apples and peanut butter and all kinds of good stuff, then hid in the trailer, where they sat all night watching.

They hadn't seen a thing, but around five a.m., they had woke him and his mom up because they'd recorded some howling and were really excited. They were going to be there again tonight, and he wished they would go away, but it was also comforting to have them there. He felt safe for once with them around.

The researchers ended up staying there for a full week, and Wasp reported that the family had come up close enough to the house one night that they had managed to get some shadowy photos of them, though you really couldn't make out much.

Wasp even came over and spent the night at my house on Friday while the researchers were still there. He acted like spending the night away from home was a really big deal, and I guess for him it was. We rented a couple of movies, and my folks had a barbecue.

Wasp acted like these were all things he had never done. I felt bad for him, yet I was kind of intrigued by his life, as it seemed way more interesting than mine. But I didn't envy him living out in the sticks with that weird family around.

Things seemed quiet on the ranch front for the next week, and then one day, Wasp made another announcement in Mr. Ramsey's class.

"Mr. Ramsey, please excuse me for being rude, but my mom just sold the ranch."

Mr. Ramsey stopped his lecture on the Mayans and asked for more details.

The whole class started interrogating Wasp, and the Mayans were relegated to history for that class session, forgotten.

Wasp was moving into town. The researchers had bought the ranch from his mom, and now Wasp and his mom were rich, he reported. They had been looking at houses and were buying one soon. His mom had quit her job as a motel maid. He was joining the basketball team. He might even be able to get a dog now.

I had never seen Wasp so happy. The entire class was happy for him, and Mr. Ramsey even had them all do a high five for Wasp.

After school that day, Wasp didn't ride the bus. His mom picked him up in a brand new Toyota car. I figured they truly had made a killing on the ranch, though I had no idea why anyone would want 30 acres of scrub woodlands with a junkyard on it.

Wasp filled me in the next day. The researchers were being funded by a rich guy who was obsessed with proving that Bigfoot existed. He knew a Bigfoot family was living on the ranch.

Wasp's mom had done a good job of habituating them, and the new owner would keep feeding them until he eventually trapped one or at least got a video of it. He was setting up everything right now, more trail cameras, feeding stations, everything.

He had paid Wasp's mom a true fortune for the place, and the two researchers would now live there full-time. They were all very excited, as they knew they would soon have a breakthrough.

I don't know what happened, but I think they probably never saw a thing. Wasp had told me the family was shy and wouldn't come out, and I suspect the Bigfoot all left shortly thereafter, as nobody ever heard a word about any Bigfoot discoveries.

Wasp and his mom bought a house not too far from mine. Wasp and I had a great friendship all through high school, and we would even camp out in my back yard, though it took me awhile to convince Wasp it was safe.

Sadly, we lost touch when we both went off to college. Wasp was class valedictorian and got a full ride to MIT, which didn't surprise me a bit. I went off to the state college and eventually became a high-school science teacher.

And even though I have a scientific bent and like evidence for things, I always try to keep an open mind, because I personally know that there are things out there that we have no idea about and can't explain.

I know because I've seen them.

About the Author

Rusty Wilson grew up in the state of Washington, in the heart of Bigfoot country. He didn't know a thing about Bigfoot until he got lost at the age of six and was then found and subsequently adopted by a kindly Bigfoot family.

He lived with them until he was 16, when they finally gave up on ever socializing him into Bigfoot ways (he hated garlic and pancakes, refused to sleep in a nest, wouldn't hunt wild pigs, and on top of it all, his feet were small).

His Bigfoot family then sent him off to Evergreen State College in nearby Olympia, thinking it would be liberal enough to take care of a kid with few redeeming qualities, plus they liked the thick foliage around the college and figured Rusty could live there, saving them money for housing.

At Evergreen, Rusty studied wildlife biology, eventually returning to the wilds, after first learning to read and write and regale everyone with his wild tales. He eventually became a flyfishing guide, and during his many travels in the wilds, he collected stories from others who have had contact with Bigfoot, also known as Sasquatch.

Because of his background, Rusty is considered to be the world's foremost Bigfoot expert (at least so by himself, if not by anyone else). He's spent many a fun evening around campfires with his clients, telling stories. Some of those clients had some pretty good stories of their own.

This is the second book of Bigfoot stories that Rusty has collected from around the campfire. If you've enjoyed this and haven't read the first, you might want to read *Rusty Wilson's Bigfoot Campfire Stories*, available at yellowcatbooks.com or amazon.com.

Whether you're a Bigfoot believer or not, we hope you enjoyed these tall tales...or are they really true stories?

Only Rusty and his fellow storytellers know for sure.

If you enjoyed this book, you will also like *The Ghost Rock Cafe* by Chinle Miller, a Bigfoot mystery. Available at yellowcatbooks.com or Amazon.com.

Made in the USA
Lexington, KY
27 January 2012